The characters and events portrayed in this book are fictitious. Any similarity to real persons, living or dead, is coincidental and not intended by the author. Any reference to real locations is only for atmospheric effect, and in no way truly represents those locations.

Published by Higher Bank Books

DAWN OF DESTRUCTION

A Post Apocalyptic EMP Thriller

WORLD WITHOUT POWER
BOOK 3

RYAN CASEY

GET A POST APOCALYPTIC NOVEL FOR FREE

To instantly receive an exclusive post apocalyptic novel totally free, sign up for Ryan Casey's author newsletter at: ryancasey books.com/fanclub

CHAPTER ONE

Sam knew something was wrong the moment Rebecca stepped through the front door.

She usually got a chippy on her way home from work on a Friday. It was their Friday thing. A bit of a tradition they had throughout their relationship. It was one of the things he missed most in the military. Not the chippy itself, of course. But the tradition. The little routine. Sitting on the sofa together, putting their feet up, and watching a shitty film on Netflix, all while tucking into a greasy, vinegar-laden fish and chips wrapped in old newspaper.

The smells of the vinegar and the old print.

The taste of salt and the richness of the batter...

And the warmth of Rebecca's body right beside him.

That's what he missed.

But he was home now. And his military days were well and truly behind him. Their fish and chip Friday tradition was back in full force.

And yet... something was different tonight.

He couldn't smell it. That's what it was. Usually, Sam smelled it the second Rebecca stepped through the front door. Usually, he heard her, too, singing away. Something he used to always roll his eyes at. But something he loved deep down.

Something he knew he'd miss if ever it went away.

Just like everything else about her.

Tonight, something was very different.

He was sitting in his usual spot: on the chair, opposite the telly, with a beer in hand. He knew it was probably too early to be drinking a beer. But fuck it. Who cared? He wasn't working at the moment. He kept on meaning to submit his CV to a few places. Nothing major. Just, like, security, that sort of thing. He hadn't worked for a while now. Not since Iraq.

Turned out nobody was mad keen on hiring a bloke who'd been under investigation for killing his superior in the army.

He sipped the beer. Felt the bubbles popping in his mouth. He knew what Rebecca would say. She'd bollock him. Tell him to get up off his arse and do something 'round the house. And she had a point. He had to admit he hadn't contributed as much these last few months. But contributing was just... well. It was difficult. Really fucking difficult.

Especially when every single time he tried to do anything productive, he was right back there again.

Back in the desert heat.

The taste of sweat constantly streaming down his face, stinging his eyes.

And the sound of crying.

Of begging.

Of—

A gunshot.

A definite gunshot.

Sam jumped. He was back in his living room again. Some replay of a football match from years ago played back on the telly. He could taste the beer on his lips again. But it wasn't appetising anymore. Wasn't enjoyable. It tasted flat. Made him feel a little sick, to be honest.

And come to think of it, he had a bit of a headache.

Shit. How many of these little bottles of cheap French beer had he knocked back?

"Sam?"

He turned around and saw Rebecca standing there in the doorway.

And then it struck him.

Fish and chips.

Only...

There were no fish and chips tonight.

Not that he could smell, anyway.

And looking at Rebecca's face, the way she was staring at him with these wide, haunted eyes... honestly, the first thing he thought was that she'd lost her job. Or that something had happened to one of her family. Maybe her mum had finally died. She'd been on the brink for a few months now. Brain tumour, end-stage. Got told she had weeks to live. That was four months ago. And she was still clinging on, her existence getting more and more painful every day. Got to the point where Rebecca was praying something'd happen to her. Something to put her out of her misery.

But... Sam wasn't sure. Something seemed different about how Rebecca was looking at him right now. Something seemed *off,* somehow.

Her eyes looked haunted.

Her face looked drained.

"Is everything okay?" he asked.

And he burped. He burped as he said it. Which felt absurd. But he tasted the alcohol and the vomit in the back of his throat, and he realised it was fitting. It was so, so fitting.

Because he realised the moment he asked the question that everything *wasn't* okay.

"Sam," Rebecca said. And he saw the tears, then—the tears streaming down her face. And even though he'd been trying not to contemplate this moment, and even though deep down he figured this moment was kind of inevitable... he still couldn't believe it was actually happening.

He felt like he was in a movie.

Like the script was pre-written, and there was nothing he could to do to intervene.

She walked towards him. Lowered her head. Like she did when she was sad and wanted a hug.

Only this time, she didn't fall into his arms.

This time, she stopped.

Like she'd walked right into an invisible wall.

Stopped right before him.

"Rebecca?" Sam said.

She looked down at the floor.

Stood there in the middle of their gorgeous cottage—the cottage they'd fought so hard to buy. The cottage they'd spent so many happy years in.

The cottage they said they were going to grow old together in.

"Rebecca," Sam said. Taking an unsteady step towards her. Realising he really was drunk. Smelling the alcohol on his breath and knocking himself sick. "What—what's—"

And then she said the words that changed everything.

She looked into his eyes and said the words that broke his world in two.

"I'm sorry," she said. "But I'm—I can't do this anymore. I..."

He didn't hear the rest of what she said.

He saw her lips moving, but he couldn't hear her.

The words just disappeared.

His ears buzzed.

He could hear explosions.

He could hear screaming.

And he could see her eyes staring at him and Yuri's eyes staring at him and blood.

Lots and lots of blood.

He stood there, and he listened to her.

Listened to what she said.

Nodded at the right moments.

And as she packed her case.

And even when she walked out of the front door and looked back at him, he just stood there.

Just watched.

Not saying a single word.

"Are you going to be okay, Sam?" she asked.

And Sam wanted to say no.

He wanted to say he wouldn't be okay.

Because she was everything to him.

And she was leaving him.

His wife was leaving him.

His love was leaving him.

He wanted to get on his knees and beg her to stay.

But instead, he stood there, took a deep breath, and nodded.

"I—I will be," he said. "I will be."

She opened her mouth.

Like she was going to say something else.

And then her mouth closed, and she nodded back at him.

"I love you," she said. "And I always will."

He didn't say "I love you" back.

And that would be the last time he saw Rebecca.

* * *

THAT WOULD BE the last time he saw Rebecca...

Until now.

Rebecca stood there, right in front of him, in the middle of this flooded road in this powerless world.

"Rebecca?" he said.

CHAPTER TWO

"Rebecca?" Sam said.

He stood in the middle of the street, and he thought he was fucking dreaming.

Because she was there. Standing right there in the road in front of him. He hadn't seen her in years. Didn't even know where she was living these days. He was pretty sure she'd left Preston at one point. Moved away.

But she was here now.

Right in front of him.

He blinked a few times. Maybe it was the lack of sleep. The exhaustion. The stress. And the fucking knife wound on his leg couldn't be helping.

But every time he opened his eyes, she was still there.

She was real.

She was here.

He wasn't imagining things at all.

"Sam," she said.

And as cheesy as it sounded, just hearing her voice again made the hairs on his arms stand right on end.

He felt his cheeks heating up. His heart racing faster. He

could feel the adrenaline kicking in and nerves taking over. He could smell sweat, and he knew it was his own. And his mouth was dry. Really, really fucking dry.

The past came rushing back. Hit him faster than a train hurtling down the track.

Standing there.

Watching her pack her stuff.

Watching her walk out the door.

Watching her leave.

Everything else around him vanished.

All his surroundings.

Suddenly, even the fact he was in a powerless world, surrounded by people he didn't know, and heading north, far away from his home, drifted into insignificance.

The only thing he saw was the woman in front of him.

The only thing that mattered was Rebecca.

"What…" he started. "How…"

But she didn't say anything.

She just stood there. Rubbing her fingers up her arms like she always did when she was nervous. It was so weird seeing her again after all these years. She didn't look any different. Maybe a little older, just slightly. But not significantly.

And it felt so familiar with all her little quirks and the little things he'd forgotten about her—like how she rubbed her arms when she was nervous. Like no time had passed at all.

And there was something else, too.

The way he felt about her the second he saw her.

The flashback of memories.

The sound of her laughter as he flicked paint on her when they were decorating the house.

Walking down a frosty country lane on a biting winter's day, holding each other's hands.

The smell of her perfume. A smell he'd forgotten up til this point.

But he could smell it now. And it brought it back. It brought it all back.

"I..." she said.

He didn't know how long they'd been standing here. Probably not as long as it felt. He wasn't sure. He didn't know what to say. Didn't know what to think.

And then he heard movement over to his right.

Looked around.

Saw Harvey trotting over to her, wagging his tail. Clearly not a very bloody good judge of character.

And then he saw the others.

He saw Wayne standing there, frowning. The kids by his side, holding his hands. Wondering what the hell was going on.

And then he saw Tara.

She was regarding him with *that* look.

A look he'd seen before. Not on her face, but on Rebecca's face in the past when she thought he was flirting with a waitress or some shit like that.

That glance at him, then over at Rebecca, and back at him again.

He remembered the kiss, and he felt a knot in his stomach tightening.

That moment of pure instinct.

Leaning over.

Kissing her.

And then...

Well.

They'd never mentioned it again since.

And now here Rebecca was.

Walking right back into his life.

And throwing his emotions into turmoil all over again.

"What're..." Rebecca started.

"What are you doing here?" he continued. Like he was

finishing Rebecca's sentence for her. Which didn't really make sense seeing as she was the one asking *him* the question.

"I... I mean, I'm..."

She stopped again. Jesus, this was getting painful. Neither of them could say a word. Both of them were completely incapacitated. And that was absolutely *not* what any of them needed right now.

"We're—we're heading north," Sam said. "The house. It's... it's not in good shape."

"Right," Rebecca said. "I mean, I was heading north too."

"Oh?"

She looked away. Then back at him. "Yeah."

He stared into her eyes for what felt like forever. And she stared back at him. It felt like he'd been lost for a while and was finally home again.

"Jesus," Wayne said, breaking the awkward silence. "You two just gonna stand there and gawk at each other, like? Or are we gonna get movin'?"

Sam lowered his head.

He cleared his throat.

He looked around at Wayne, and at Tara again, who stood there, her gaze still interchanging between him and Rebecca, again and again.

And then he looked up at Rebecca.

"I mean... If you're heading north, and we're heading north. I guess... I guess it kind of makes sense to... to both head north. Right?"

She looked at him. Right into his eyes again.

And a part of him expected to wake up.

A part of him still thought this was a dream.

A part of him expected her to start laughing at him and telling him to get fucked.

Or to pull out a knife and start stabbing him.

But then something else happened.

Something... worse, somehow.

Two people walked out from behind the car to the side of the road and the side of Rebecca.

A man. Well-built. Salt and pepper grey. Handsome.

And holding his hand... a boy.

A little boy.

"Sam," Rebecca said. "This... this is Tristan. And—and this here is Leonard. My—my son."

CHAPTER THREE

Sam couldn't get over how fucking weird today was turning out to be.

A bloke was standing in front of him. By Rebecca's side. He didn't understand. Not at first. Not for that initial split second, where all his problems drifted off into the background, and nothing else seemed to matter. Nothing but the fact his ex-wife was right here in front of him.

And then it clicked.

He saw the bloke and the little kid by his side, and it clicked.

The bloke was tall. Well-built. Muscular. Similar physique to Sam's a few years ago before he slacked a little bit. He didn't look much like Sam otherwise. Looked kind of... well. Kind of corporate. Like he had a layer of grease smothered over him. His hair was slicked back, with little specks of white and grey. He had this smile on his face. A smile that pissed Sam off right away.

And then he saw the kid standing right beside him, and any doubts he had about who this might be disappeared.

The kid looked just like Rebecca. Well, the male equivalent of Rebecca. Same brown eyes. Same curly hair. And that same cheeky, shy smile that Rebecca used to have.

He remembered the first time he'd met Rebecca at Cleo's Halloween party. Shitty party. He wasn't even gonna go. But a couple of his mates at the time kept pestering him to go along, and sometimes it's better just to go along and spare yourself the bullshit.

He remembered walking in dressed in all black. People kept asking who he'd come as, so he said Batman. A few people found it funny. Most people were too pissed or high to get the joke.

He'd seen Cleo and a few of the other lads, and he was just finishing sipping his shitty lager, getting ready to go home and turn in now he'd shown his face, when he saw her at the other side of the room.

And it was like one of those clichéd moments in a movie. Eyes meeting across the floor of a party. And she had this look on her face. This smile on her face.

And although he wasn't a romantic, he knew instantly that he couldn't ignore her.

So he said "fuck it" to his inhibitions, and he walked over to her.

The rest, as they say, was history.

And now here he was.

Rebecca.

Her fella, Tristan.

And her son.

Leonard.

"Tristan," Rebecca said. Clearly finding this whole thing just as awkward as Sam. "This—this is Sam. My... my ex-husband."

And Sam half-expected Tristan to punch him in the face or something. What was the etiquette when meeting your wife's ex? Fucked if he knew.

But instead, something kind of crazy happened.

Tristan's smile widened.

He stretched out a hand, walking towards Sam.

"Sam," Tristan said. "I've heard a hell of a lot about you. Pleasure to meet you."

Whoa. That was not what Sam expected. To be honest, he wasn't sure how to feel about it. He preferred the idea of him being an utter dick, giving Sam enough reason to hate him.

But here he was.

Standing here.

Beaming.

Hand outstretched.

Not a glimmer of nervousness in his eyes.

Sam glanced at Tara, then back at Tristan.

And he lowered his head and shook his hand.

"Hopefully all good stuff she's told you," Sam said.

Tristan shook Sam's hand with *just* the right amount of force. He laughed. "Oh, of course. Absolutely blinding review."

Sam tried to pull his hand away, but this bloke was still holding on to it, laughing still, too. Like he'd just said the funniest thing in the world.

Besides, he didn't know how genuine he was being. Had Rebecca been kind about him? Or was he being sarcastic?

Fuck. What the hell did it matter, really?

Tristan finally released his hand.

And that's when Sam saw the kid standing there.

Staring up at him.

Hands behind his back.

Cheeky look on his little face.

"This here's Leonard," Tristan said. Speaking to Sam like he was his best frigging mate or something. "I call him Leo sometimes. But Rebecca isn't so keen."

Sam stood before this kid and felt something weird in the middle of his chest. A weird hole opening up. An emptiness.

A kid that could have been his and Rebecca's.

An alternate life he could've lived.

Like he was looking through a window at how things could've been.

He held out a hand.

"Hi, little man," he said.

Leonard glanced down at Sam's outstretched hand.

And then, somewhat reluctantly, he took it and shook it.

Sam stood there in the middle of this road shaking hands with his ex-wife's kid while his wife's new fella waffled on over-enthusiastically about any old shite.

He stood there, and he looked at Rebecca.

And the way she looked back at him... it was like no time had passed at all since she'd walked away.

Since she'd left.

It was like they were still in that moment.

Like it had never gone away.

Never ended.

He looked at Rebecca—looked into this peephole to the past—and then he took a deep breath.

"This... this here's Harvey. My dog."

"Never had you down as a dog man," Rebecca said.

"People can change," Sam said.

Rebecca smiled. "Apparently so."

She held eye contact for just a little too long. A little longer than felt comfortable.

Sam looked away. Cleared his throat. "This here... This is Tara."

Rebecca looked at Tara, then back at Sam, and at Tara again.

"We met on the road. I helped her."

Tara puffed out her lips. Narrowed her eyes. "Umm, I kind of helped you too."

"Yeah. Sure. I..."

Shit. He knew there was a reason he hated introductions.

He watched Tara walk over to Rebecca.

Watched her say hi to her.

Beaming smile across her face. A little bit too smiley, if anything.

And then he looked over at Wayne.

Wayne and the kids.

"And this... this is Wayne. Wayne, Marky, Millie."

Wayne didn't say anything. He just nodded. He was clearly confused about everything going on here.

"So," Tristan said. "Now we've got the pleasantries over. You said you were heading north?"

Sam nodded. Couldn't quite look Tristan in the eye. "Tara's... Tara's got family up in Arnside."

"Arnside?" Tristan said. "Lovely place."

"Thanks," Tara said. "I kind of hate it."

"Oh," Tristan said, looking a little flummoxed. "I..."

An awkward silence hung in the air.

A silence that Sam knew needed filling.

"Well," he said. "I guess—I guess none of us want to stand around here any longer."

"A-men to that," Wayne said.

He looked at Rebecca.

At Tristan.

At little Leonard, staring up with that cheeky grin.

"Well," he said. "I guess we'd... I guess we'd better get going. Right?"

And even though it felt like there was so much more to say, even though it felt like there were so many more things to address... now wasn't the moment.

"Yes," Tristan said. "I think that'd be a very good idea."

Sam looked at Rebecca.

She looked back at him.

And then he took a deep breath, and he turned away.

It was time for this awkward as fuck journey to begin.

If only he had any idea what awaited on the road ahead.

CHAPTER FOUR

One thing Tara would never get used to?

Waking up naturally without the aid of an alarm clock.

Reaching over for her phone and realising she not only didn't *have* a phone, but even if she did, it wasn't working.

Oh. And waking up somewhere other than by Jonno's side.

That was something of a perk of the new world, at least.

She opened her eyes and stared up at the mouldy ceiling. It was cold in here. So cold that she was shivering. She wasn't sure whether it was cold outside. It was probably August—or rather, September now, so it shouldn't be too chilly just yet. They were still well within summer's umbrella. If there were such a thing as central heating still, it'd be nowhere near switched on just yet.

She was lying on a creaky old bed, and her back ached like mad. She'd tossed and turned all night in these damp, smelly sheets. Convinced herself she was never going to doze off. Which, ironically, usually helped her doze off.

But honestly, as much as she knew she needed sleep, a part of her didn't want to close her eyes.

She didn't want to see the memory of what'd happened replaying in her mind all over again.

She didn't want to see Jonno standing there in front of her.

Tears in his eyes.

Gun to her head.

She didn't want to hear the sound of that gunshot.

The explosion she thought would be the last thing she heard.

And she didn't want to taste that blood again.

Rusty metal on her lips.

A taste she wasn't ever going to forget.

But she had.

She'd fallen asleep, and she'd relived it all over again.

The sound of the gunshot.

The taste of blood.

And those eyes.

Those eyes staring up at her.

Vacant on the floor.

Sitting in a lump of exploded brain.

His skull, cracked and jagged, like an Easter egg that'd just been rolled down a hill.

She swallowed a sickly lump in her throat and felt weak, but she wasn't all that hungry. It was quiet in this bedroom. Quiet, but for the ringing in her ears. A ringing that'd started with that gunshot in the cellar.

She always thought she had tinnitus. She used to complain to Jonno about how her ears rang sometimes and how she wanted to go to the doctor and get them syringed.

But he was always... reluctant to let her go.

He'd always find another plan for them for that day.

And then he'd tell her she didn't have to worry about it. That she was imagining things. That she was just fine.

She saw it for what it was now. She was stupid and naive not to see it for what it was at the time.

Or... well. She *had* seen it for what it was.

She just fooled herself over how much control she really had over her life.

But he was gone now.

He was gone, and she was free.

The blood.

The brain.

The skull...

She tasted vomit in her mouth, strong and bitter.

Was she free? Really?

Or was she just in a different kind of prison?

She got up. Looked around this bedroom. It was a house on the A6 up towards Lancaster. Clearly empty. Which made it less of a moral dilemma to break into and sleep in for the night. They'd walked through a few villages on the way up and seen the familiar sights: cars abandoned. Shops looted. Some people walking the waterlogged streets in the hope of salvation. Others locking their doors and praying they had enough supplies to get them through before help arrived.

If help arrived.

Because surely people realised by now that help wasn't on its way?

A week had passed since the blackout. Three days since Tara and the others ran into Rebecca, Sam's ex, on the road.

It'd been a weird few days. After the craziness of the first few days, the last few had been kind of... well, uneventful.

Their focus had been solely on heading north.

And they hadn't even had much to say about it.

They'd walked in separate groups. Wayne and the kids, Millie and Marky, who, to be fair to them, actually seemed quite sweet.

Rebecca, her husband, Tristan, and their son, Leonard, obviously stuck together.

And Tara walked with Sam.

Only Sam seemed... distant. Which went without saying, right? His ex-wife had appeared out of nowhere with a husband

and a kid he had no idea existed. That shit was bound to be hard to swallow.

But at the same time—and as shitty as the timing was—she wanted to talk to him.

About that kiss on the road.

She remembered how it made her feel. Not to be cringy, but yes, she'd felt butterflies.

But he hadn't said anything about it since. And it was almost a week ago. And sure, they'd been distracted. They'd had other things on their mind.

But she just wanted him to acknowledge it.

She just wanted him to tell her it meant something.

Did it mean something?

Did it mean anything at all?

She looked in the dusty mirror. The room was dark, but she looked like shit. She was pale. Looked like she'd aged about a decade in the last week.

And was that a speck of blood on her cheek?

She rubbed her cheek. Heart rate picking up.

She didn't want any trace of Jonno on her.

She didn't want any reminders.

Of Jonno.

Or of...

No.

Don't think of that.

Don't go there.

She took a deep breath of the cool air. She was going to stay strong. She was going to keep her shit together. There was a real chance she would make it to Arnside today—and it likely meant a reunion with her parents.

She wasn't sure what they'd think when she turned up with a bunch of strangers. No, actually, she was sure: they were going to fucking hate it.

But maybe they wouldn't have to go there anyway.

Maybe they'd find somewhere else along the way. An alternative. Because they weren't heading north *solely* because Tara had family up there. Sam said something about a campsite up that way. And how being as far away from any major cities as possible was also a bonus.

But it felt like Tara was being drawn back home.

Out of one prison and into another...

And she was only just beginning to taste freedom.

She stood at the mirror, and she took another deep breath.

Tied her hair up.

She was going to go out of this bedroom.

And she was going to face the day.

She stepped out of the bedroom and into the relative brightness of the landing.

She hoped today was just as uneventful as the last few, all things considered.

Her prayers weren't going to be answered.

CHAPTER FIVE

Okay, so Sam wasn't as good a chef as he liked to think. That's something he'd learned this last week.

He stood in the backyard of the house they'd stayed in overnight. The garden was overgrown. The grass was so long. There was an old trampoline in the back corner, all torn in the middle. A deflated football sat on its side, and there was one of those swingball stands, too. He used to love playing swingball as a kid. Summers in the garden at his grandparents' caravan site. Whacking that ball again and again while his granddad laughed along every time it hit Sam. He was competitive, his old granddad. It was a family trait. Not always the most attractive or endearing trait, Sam was sure.

But you know what?

If it kept him alive, then there was something to be said for competitiveness.

He'd made a barbecue out of an old steel drum. Found a load of old coal at a petrol station and tossed some wood in there too. It was really smoky, catching in his lungs. And whatever was in this metal drum before did not smell good.

And neither did the can of chunky chicken sitting on top of it, bubbling away.

He knew it was a rogue choice for breakfast. But they had a long day ahead and needed to get their energy levels up as much as possible. Chicken and rice was pretty much the staple meal, even if it was out of a can.

No. *Especially* if it was out of a can.

There wasn't going to be much fresh chicken going around anymore.

He looked down into the fire, crackling away beneath him. Felt the heat rising towards his face. He still felt sore after all the shit he'd been through a couple of days ago. The beatings. The collapse down the stairs.

And his ears, too.

His ears wouldn't stop ringing after Jonno fired the bullet that ended his own life.

He kept on thinking about how horrifying that moment was.

The blood splattering everywhere.

Chunks of brain clinging to his cellar walls.

It was grim for him to witness. So for Tara... yeah, that shit didn't bear thinking about.

He hoped she was okay. She hadn't said a lot in the last few days. Seemed... distant, somehow. Which was odd for her.

And to be honest, Sam had been kind of distracted and distant too.

Because the small matter of his ex-wife, her new fella, and their son walking back into his life had sort of destabilised him a little bit.

He looked down at that pale, anaemic pan of chicken in sauce bubbling away beneath him. He didn't know why he was so surprised that Rebecca had moved on with her life. They'd split up years ago, and they were both still pretty young.

But he'd kind of buried the possibility in his mind. He'd tried to ignore what he knew was inevitable and what he knew was likely.

And then just seeing them appear out of nowhere...

Yeah. It wasn't weird to feel a little bit uncomfortable about that. A little bit on edge about that.

There were all sorts of shit he wanted to say to her. All kinds of questions he wanted to ask her.

But in the end, he didn't say a thing.

In the end, he just walked.

Kept his head down. Small-talked when he had to. Disappeared at every opportunity.

Because, sure, he *wanted* to talk.

But at the same time, he felt afraid.

Afraid of what she might say.

And afraid of how he might feel.

He heard footsteps approaching. Two sets of footsteps. One of them was quite clearly Harvey.

He turned around, expecting Tara, when he saw someone he didn't expect.

It was Rebecca.

Rebecca stood there with her arms wrapped around her chest.

She walked towards Sam, doing that awkward half-smile fucking *everyone* does when they're feeling uncomfortable.

"Something smells good," she said.

Sam cleared his throat, a knot tightening in his stomach. "Don't lie to me."

"Okay. Something smells gross."

"That's... that's more like it."

He stood there, Rebecca by his side, and he stared at the bubbling chicken stew.

"So," Rebecca said. "I slept terribly."

"Right."

"Tristan's... Tristan's a big leg-twitcher. Seriously, he must run an absolute marathon in his sleep or something. Never stops."

Sam didn't know what to say. But he realised he didn't feel... well, *comfortable*.

Talking with Rebecca was a surreal reality he was still getting used to.

Especially about her new fella's sleeping habits.

"Tara seems nice," Rebecca said.

"What?"

"Tara. She... she seems a nice woman. Chatted a few times."

"Yeah. She's... she's a good person."

An awkward silence hung in the air between them.

And Sam just wanted to run away.

He wanted to get back inside the house, and he wanted to get away from Rebecca.

Away from here.

"I feel like... like you and me haven't talked at all, though."

Sam cleared his throat again. His face felt hot, and he was beginning to sweat. "What is there to say?"

"I mean, it's been years since I last saw you—"

"You left me," Sam said.

Rebecca's face turned then. "You still hold that against me? After—after everything we went through?"

He looked into her eyes, and he felt bad right away. 'Cause she was right. He could hardly blame her for walking away. Especially after what he'd become.

But he just... He couldn't *express* himself.

He couldn't say the words he wanted to say.

He wanted to tell her that Tristan seemed a decent bloke.

And that Leonard seemed a good kid.

He wanted so much to exorcise any bitterness he felt and wish the woman he'd loved more than anyone in his entire life the very best.

He opened his mouth and went to speak when suddenly he heard the back door swing open.

Wayne came running out.

He looked worried. Very fucking worried.

"Marky," he said.

"Everything okay?" Rebecca asked.

"It's—it's Marky," he said. "He's... he's gone."

CHAPTER SIX

Wayne knew something was wrong the second he opened his eyes.

He'd had some really shitty dreams. Dreams that he was back home. Dreams that he was lying there in his and Carly's flat. Only... something was off. The bedroom door was open. And he could hear footsteps out there.

Footsteps dragging along the hallway.

Getting closer, and closer, and closer...

He lay there frozen in bed. He could smell something. Something that smelled like rot. It reminded him of when he was a kid. He went on work experience with his dad at the tip Granddad worked at. Place where people went to dump their rubbish. The people there treated Granddad like shit. Everyone treated *everyone* like shit there.

But Granddad always said he did the job to put food on the table. Didn't matter if it was a glamorous job or not. He did what he had to do to support those he loved. To support his family.

Wayne would never forget the stench of the rubbish.

The sight of those maggots crawling on the outside of the rubbish bag.

And something in there.

Something... furry.

He'd later find out it was a bunch of dead puppies. He heard Granddad saying about it to Mum. All of them had been found, drowned.

Nobody knew who'd drowned those puppies. Or why. Probably a puppy farm on the brink of being rumbled.

But that memory always stuck with Wayne.

That *stench* always stuck with Wayne.

He heard the footsteps creaking along the hallway.

Saw the shadow getting closer.

Heard a cracking sound.

Cracking that sounded like...

Bones.

"Wayne..." a voice gasped. Hoarse.

And getting closer.

Getting closer and closer.

And he couldn't get up.

He couldn't move.

He could only lie there, frozen to the spot.

Watching that shadow get closer.

Listening to those dragged, cracking footsteps get closer.

And listening to that hoarse voice inching closer...

"Wayne..."

He tried to close his eyes, but he couldn't.

He tried to tilt his head away, but he couldn't.

He could hear flies buzzing around.

So many flies.

Some of them bumping into him.

Headbutting him.

And then he heard it stop.

The footsteps stopped.

The creaking stopped.

All of it stopped.

He lay there. Heart racing. Chest tight.

Staring at the door out onto the hallway.

And he could see the shape of the shadow.

He could see the shape of that shadow, and he knew who it was.

He knew it was Carly.

He knew he was going to see her again in that awful state.

He tried to close his eyes.

He tried to turn his head away.

He tried, and he tried.

But he couldn't.

He looked at that hallway door and waited for her to enter when suddenly he felt something cold on his arm.

He looked down and saw a hand holding onto his arm.

A little hand.

A blackened, decaying hand.

And then he saw Marky and Millie.

Pale-faced.

Rotting flesh.

Skeletal.

Maggots and flies all over them.

But smiling.

Both of them smiling.

"You promised," that hoarse voice said.

Wayne swung around, and he saw her then.

Right at the foot of the bed.

Towering over him.

She was pale. And she was covered in blood.

Pale, covered in blood, and also bombarded with flies.

She didn't look happy.

She looked *evil*.

"Carly—"

"You promised you wouldn't let them down."

"And I won't."

But then her hand stretched out.

Grabbed his mouth.

Hard.

It was so cold and slimy. He could feel things falling out of it. Falling out of her palm and into his mouth.

And as he lay there and they stared down at him, he could only look up in horror as he realised what it was.

Exactly what it was.

Maggots.

"You promised," Carly said.

Wayne tried to shout.

He tried to scream.

He tried to *promise*.

But his mouth was sealed shut.

And he was pinned down.

And maggots were filling his mouth, more and more and more.

Carly looked down into his eyes. Crying tears of blood.

"Don't let them down," she said.

Wayne shook his head.

And then Carly leaned in closer.

Leaned in with that putrid breath.

Her hair all patchy.

Her skull on show, all red and bloodied.

"Don't let *me* down."

Wayne shook his head again.

She held him there.

Held him there, pinned down, as worms started to ooze out of her lips alongside a thick, black fluid.

And then she smiled.

Some of that black fluid seeping between the cracks in her teeth.

"Good," she said.

And then she pulled her hand away and leaned in with that

wormy, gungey mouth, and she pressed her lips against his as worms slithered out all down his throat and—

He jolted upright.

He was in a lounge somewhere. A lounge he didn't recognise. The torn curtains were closed, and light was peeking in through them. The old-fashioned carpet was dusty and stained. And the sofa he was on was so, so uncomfortable.

And then it came to him. It all came back to him.

The journey.

The journey north.

Needing to rest for the night.

Finding this place.

And...

He looked over at the other sofa on the other side of the room and saw something that made him catch his breath a little.

Millie.

She was lying there under the blanket.

Eyes closed.

Snoring away.

He smiled when he saw her. Smiled and almost fucking cried.

She was strong.

So, so strong.

If it wasn't for her, he wasn't sure how he would've made it this far.

If it wasn't for her, he had no idea how he'd've looked after Marky.

Marky.

Wait...

He stood up.

Staggered over to the sofa.

"Marky?" he said.

But the closer he got to the sofa, the more he realised his worst fears were coming true.

"Ma... Marky," he muttered.

Because where Marky was—where he'd fallen to sleep—there was no Marky.

Marky was gone.

Immediately, he ran out of the lounge.

Almost tumbled over on his way.

He saw Sam in the garden. Sam and Rebecca.

He ran through the kitchen, out towards them.

And all he could say?

"Marky!"

Sam turned around.

Rebecca turned around.

They both frowned at him.

"Everything okay?"

And then Wayne said the words that turned his blood cold.

"It's—it's Marky. He's... he's gone."

CHAPTER SEVEN

"It's Marky. He's—he's gone."

"Gone?" Sam said. "What do you mean he's gone?"

"He's—he's not in the house. He's... He's gone. Something—something's happened to him."

Sam stood in the garden opposite Rebecca. The chicken stew cooking over the makeshift barbecue was bubbling over, burning at the edges. It smelled sour. Unappetising. Knocked him sick, to be honest.

And seeing Wayne standing here, pale-faced, clearly terrified... yeah, that didn't exactly help either.

Sam could hear him breathing rapidly, shakily. Behind him, he saw more figures emerge. Millie. Leonard. And then Tristan and Faye followed, all trying to figure out what was going on here.

"What's happened?" Tristan asked.

"It's—it's my lad," Wayne said, staggering around the water-logged garden. "He's... he's... Marky!"

He shouted really loud, his voice echoing in the silence. Up above, a few birds flew away, flapping away from the noise.

And Sam really didn't know what to say. Or what to think.

"Are—are you sure he's—"

"Am I *sure?*" Wayne said, squaring up to Sam. "Am I fucking *sure?* He was—he was right there. Right there on the sofa, next to Millie. And—and I woke up and he's... he's gone."

Sam raised a hand. "I'm just trying to rule everything out, okay? Before... before we start thinking about..."

He didn't want to say it.

Wayne and Millie had been through enough already.

But the possibility that Marky had gone—for whatever reason —was looking pretty fucking ominous right now.

"Tara. Tristan. You two... you two search the house. Wayne, keep a close eye on the kids."

"On—on the kids? If my boy's out there, I'm not fucking leaving him."

"Rebecca and I will... We'll search the street. And if we don't find him... then you can look yourself. But for now, Millie needs you. Okay? Millie needs you. So watch her. Watch her and watch Leonard. And we'll be back here in no time with your boy. Okay?"

Wayne shook his head. He looked like he wanted to argue. Looked like he wanted to fight.

And then he quite visibly deflated.

"Just find him. Okay? Find him."

Sam nodded.

He looked at Rebecca.

Then he looked at the trees behind the house.

The trees in the garden. It was so overgrown. He remembered hearing Marky say something about it last night. How it looked like it was full of secrets, or something like that. He definitely loved how overgrown the garden was. And he was definitely interested in what was in the trees behind the house.

So it made sense that he might be out there.

Right?

"Marky!" Sam called.

His voice echoed through the woods as he clambered his way over a load of long, thick branches. The grass was so tall, right up to his knees. It wasn't raining anymore, but it felt damp in here. He could smell the dampness in the air. And he could taste it, too. A reminder of what it used to be like wild camping with Rebecca.

Wild camping with the woman beside him right now.

He looked at her.

She looked back at him.

Neither of them saying another word.

Neither of them finishing their conversation from earlier.

Just both so focused on one task.

Finding Marky.

He climbed over more of these overgrown branches and leaves. There were so many of them, the damp fingers of bushes trailing against Sam's face. Back at the house, he could still hear shouting. "*Marky! Marky!*" So they hadn't found him. When it went quiet, *then* he could think about heading back. *Then* he could think about giving up the search.

But the more time passed, the more it looked like the worst was true.

That Marky was gone.

He didn't know where, but he was gone.

He walked further down the slope and into the foliage when he saw something up ahead.

It was a cabin.

An old cabin, right in the midst of all this foliage.

The windows were all steamed up and covered in condensation. But they were intact.

And there was something else, too.

The door.

The door was ajar.

And it was swinging.

He nudged Rebecca, and then he nodded ahead.

She squinted over where he was pointing, and then her eyes widened.

"There," Sam said. "Has to be."

They stood there, together, and Sam couldn't help admitting something.

He was afraid.

Afraid of what he might find.

Because it looked like there was somebody in the cabin.

Or if there wasn't someone in the cabin right now, someone had been in the place recently.

A theory further proved by the muddy prints beneath him.

He stood there. His throat completely dry.

Totally in the clutches of fear.

And then he tightened his fists, and he walked slowly towards that cabin.

The closer he got to it, the darker everything seemed to become.

The thicker the branches seemed to grow.

The more the sky hid behind the clouds above.

He kept on walking.

Kept on getting closer.

And for a second, as he got closer, he swore he felt Rebecca's hand brush against his.

He stood outside the cabin door.

Saw the darkness inside.

Smelled the damp and the mould of this rotten old cabin.

"Marky?" he said.

He pulled the door open.

Stepped inside.

Heart racing.

Time standing still.

He stepped further into the cabin.

Onto the creaky wooden floorboards.

He felt cobwebs clinging to his face.

Saw movement in the corners of the cabin.

And then, as he stepped further inside, he saw something that both terrified him and filled him with hope for a moment.

"Marky," he said. "It's…"

And then he stopped.

He stopped because it wasn't Marky.

It wasn't Marky at all.

It was a doll.

A life-sized doll of a child.

A ventriloquist's dummy.

Smiling at Sam.

Only…

"Creepy," Rebecca said. "I hate those things."

But Sam couldn't speak.

He couldn't say a word.

Because as he got closer to the dummy, he realised something horrifying.

"Sam?" Rebecca said. "He's—he's not here."

"He's not," Sam said, touching the dummy's shoulder. "But he has been."

Rebecca frowned. "What?"

"Just… just look."

Rebecca squinted.

And then her eyes widened.

"Oh," she said.

And in that instant, Sam knew she understood too.

She'd seen it too.

And she was just as terrified as he was.

CHAPTER EIGHT

Marky wanted to see the jungle at the bottom of the garden, especially when he saw the lady with the light out there.

It was dark, but he couldn't sleep properly. Millie kept snoring. He tried pushing her and waking her up, but she was fast asleep. So then he'd climbed over her and gone out into the kitchen because he didn't like the fireplace in the living room 'cause it looked like monsters might come out of it.

He kept thinking monsters were in there.

That they were going to climb out and eat him and take him away.

So he just wanted to go for a walk in the creepy old house and have a look around, like he was an explorer. A brave explorer.

He used to play games like that with Mummy. Pretend he was exploring the jungle, and she'd pretend to be exploring with him until they saw something scary, and then she'd tickle him and laugh, and he'd scream and cry and laugh too. He missed Mummy. He missed her a lot.

And he knew Millie said she was still there in his heart or whatever, but it wasn't as good.

He missed her lots.

So he walked out into the hallway. He felt cold. Shaky. He kept on thinking he saw things moving, but he knew it was probably just the weird floaty things in his eyes. The things that danced in front of his eyes when he was tired. They scared him sometimes, but Mummy always told him not to be scared of anything 'cause she would always be here to look after him and protect him.

But she wasn't here anymore.

She was gone.

And he really wanted to see her again.

He walked over to the big glass doors at the back of the house. He knew he shouldn't. Wayne wouldn't be happy if he knew he was walking around. But it would be okay. He was strong, and he was brave, and he was a tough adventurer. That's what Mummy always used to say. Her brave little soldier.

He was a soldier, and he was going to get her back.

He was *her* soldier, and he was going to find her.

He stood at the glass and looked out into the dark. He couldn't see anything out there. The old trampoline, which didn't work. The trees, with their big black branches in the sky. Moving in the wind.

The more he looked out there, the more he wanted to go out.

To go out there and go into the trees and explore.

But then he knew he should get some sleep because if he didn't, he might get told off.

He went to turn around when he saw something.

The light.

Right at the bottom of the garden.

He stood still. Looked at that light. It was weird. He hadn't seen a light for a bit. The adults kept going on about the light and the power, and he didn't really understand.

But right now, he saw this light.

Shining at him.

And then...

And then he saw the person holding the light.

He saw them turn the light up.

Point it at their face.

It was a lady.

He saw her sitting there in the grass, wearing a white dress, and she was smiling.

She looked nice.

Looked friendly.

And she was holding something too.

Something that looked like...

A toy?

Holding it out.

Waving it at him.

And then the light went out, and the lady disappeared.

He stood there at the windows. He didn't know what to do. He knew he should go back to the sofa and curl up next to Millie. But Millie was smelly, and he didn't want to sleep next to her.

And then this lady.

With the toy.

She looked so smiley.

She looked so nice.

He looked back. Back towards the corridor.

And then he turned around to the glass.

He could just go have a look.

He could just see.

He reached for the handle.

Opened it.

He had to pull it really hard, and he thought he wouldn't make it.

But eventually, it moved.

It shifted open.

And he was outside.

He kept it open. Walked out across the squelchy ground.

And the closer he got to where he'd seen the lady, the further he got down the grass, he realised he couldn't see her anymore.

It was windy. Really windy.

And it was cold, too.

So cold.

He looked back. Over at that door.

It'd swung to now. Made him jump when it did.

He should go back.

Go back home.

He turned around, and he saw her again.

She was right there in the bushes.

That torch in her hand.

The toy in the other hand.

Smiling at him.

She lifted the toy and waved.

And he waved back at her.

She nodded her head back. Like she was trying to get him to follow.

And he felt... he felt like he wasn't sure.

Just that he wanted this toy.

And he wanted a new friend.

A secret new friend at the bottom of the garden.

A new mummy.

He looked back again.

Then he turned around and walked towards that lady.

Only...

The light had gone again.

The lady had gone again.

He walked further to the bottom of the garden.

Dragged himself through the branches, which scratched his face.

He just wanted to get to the lady.

To find her.

Why was she hiding from him?

He really wanted that toy, whatever it was.

He got on his knees and climbed under a few of the other branches. He could feel the cold water seeping through his legs as rain started to fall heavily from above. Wayne was going to be so mad at him. He was soaking wet. He was going to know he'd gone out of the house, and he was going to tell him off, even though he was usually always nice to him.

He climbed up, wiping the mud and the smelly stuff off his jeans, and then he looked ahead.

He could see something in the distance.

A little shed.

There was a light on in there.

And the door was open.

He stood there in the rain.

Stood there, shaking.

He looked back over his shoulder.

Then over at the shed again.

And then he smiled.

This was like his own little adventure.

Mummy would be so proud of him.

He was so strong.

Her little soldier.

He took a deep breath.

And then he walked towards the light of that shed.

What was the worst that could happen?

* * *

HE DIDN'T SEE the figure standing there in the trees.

Watching.

CHAPTER NINE

Wayne had no idea how fucking long he'd been searching the house from top to bottom when he saw them both standing at the bottom of the garden.

It was bright outside. It hadn't rained for a few days, but the garden was still waterlogged. That grass was so tall. He wondered if maybe Marky was just hiding in there, playing one of his games. He used to love pretending he was someplace else. Pretending he was exploring the world or pretending he was an astronaut up in space.

He pictured him crouched in the grass, crawling through, hiding from the "dinosaurs" like he was in Jurassic Park.

He wanted that to be the case.

He wanted that so much.

It was quiet outside. The only sounds he could hear were the birds singing above and the gentle breeze brushing those tall, overgrown tree branches at the bottom of the garden against each other. It made him feel sick just looking at those trees. He'd heard Marky mentioning how he wanted to go exploring in there. How it looked like a rainforest. And Wayne... Wayne should've noticed that glint in his eye. He should've known Marky was a curious kid.

But he didn't expect him to walk away.

To disappear.

He was a good kid. Curious, but good.

He wouldn't just disappear in the middle of the night.

Would he?

The chicken stew cooking outside smelled sour and burned now. It made Wayne feel even sicker.

Reminded him of the sourness of Carly's body, lying there on their bed, a damp patch beneath her.

A memory that made his head spin.

That made him want to vomit.

He took a deep, shaky breath, trying to keep himself composed, trying to keep shit under control, when he saw them both standing at the bottom of the garden.

Sam.

Rebecca.

They were both alone.

There was no Marky with them.

And they...

The way they were looking at Wayne.

The way they were looking right into his eyes.

It made everything around him disappear.

The house.

The trees.

Everything.

All he saw were Sam and Rebecca.

"Where—where is he?" he said, staggering out of the house, splashing across the flooded concrete patio.

Sam didn't say anything.

Rebecca didn't say anything.

They just looked at him with this awful look on their faces.

A look that could mean so many things.

A look that could mean they hadn't found him

Or a look that could mean they had.

Only the news wasn't good.

Wayne stumbled further across the grass, getting closer to them.

"Where—where is he? Did you—did you find him?"

Sam looked at Rebecca, and Rebecca looked back at him.

"Answer me!" Wayne shouted.

"I... We didn't find him," Sam said.

Relief.

A blast of relief.

'Cause if they hadn't found him, that meant... that meant he wasn't necessarily dead.

At least he was still alive.

And then, after that initial relief, Wayne felt something else.

Fear.

Because if they hadn't found him... he was gone.

And there was something else, too.

A feeling he had.

A feeling Sam and Rebecca weren't telling him everything.

"What?" Wayne said.

Sam looked back at him. He looked pale and tired. Haunted, even.

"We found something," Rebecca said.

"What do you mean you found something?"

"There's... there's a cabin out there. In the woods. And we—"

Wayne didn't even think.

He didn't hesitate.

Not for a second.

He ran past them towards the bottom of the garden.

"Wayne!"

He didn't stop.

He kept on running.

Clambered past the overgrown bushes.

Scraped his way through those long branches, which scratched at his ankles and clawed at his face.

He pushed, and he pushed until he was through to the other side as the others chased after him.

Desperate for him not to see whatever was in there.

Eager for him not to find what they'd found.

He climbed over a small bush when he saw it.

A cabin.

A little cabin, right at the bottom of the garden.

It looked old. The wood was all rotten and covered in moss.

And the door was open.

He felt his fists tense up.

"I'm coming," he said. "I'm—I'm not leaving you behind."

And then he ran across the muddy ground towards that cabin.

"Wayne," Sam shouted. "It's—We don't know what it means, okay? We don't know what it means. Not—not yet."

But Wayne was already climbing the creaky wooden steps.

He was already stepping inside the cabin.

He was already through the door.

He stood there in the cabin. It smelled damp. And there was another smell in the air, too. A weird sweetness. Like... like stale vomit.

He looked around this dusty cabin, past the mass of cobwebs, and then he saw him.

Sitting right there.

Staring back at him.

"Ma—Marky?"

He stepped closer and then he realised something.

It wasn't Marky at all.

It was some weird doll.

A dummy.

Like a ventriloquist's dummy, only the biggest one he'd ever seen.

Only...

"Wayne," Sam said. He was at the door now. So too, was Rebecca.

But Wayne didn't hear anything.

All he saw were the clothes this dummy was wearing.

The little blue jeans, torn at the knees.

The black hoodie with the Manchester United logo.

Wayne stood and stared at the dummy, and he felt like he was sinking into a hole beneath him.

Because this dummy.

This dummy was wearing Marky's clothes.

CHAPTER TEN

Sam stood in the dark, dingy kitchen of the derelict old house and tried to figure out what the hell to say or what the hell to do next.

Because what the hell was he supposed to say or do?

Little Marky had gone missing. And not only that but his clothes had been found in some creepy cabin at the bottom of the garden, wrapped over a terrifying ventriloquist's dummy.

And as much as he tried to tell himself that maybe there was an innocent explanation... he knew for a fact he was being naive.

They were dealing with a weirdo.

And he was very, very worried about Marky.

Wayne was pacing around the kitchen, rubbing the sides of his sweaty face. He smelled of body odour, which cut through the damp stench of this abandoned house. His eyes were wide, and he looked a man possessed. Sam felt bad for him. Really fucking bad. He'd never had a kid, but the thought of losing one... that was a pain that everyone could picture. The worst pain imaginable.

Everyone in here was silent. Tara. Rebecca. Tristan. Even Leonard was quiet.

And poor little Millie.

She just stood there. Head lowered. Tears soaking her cheeks.

She was such a strong kid. Sam had seen that for himself already. Mature, far beyond her years.

But now, she looked like a child.

She looked vulnerable.

Like the act of being strong for her little brother, even after all the shit she'd been through, had slipped.

"We—we can't just fucking stand around in here," Wayne said. "Doing nothing. We—we need to be out there. *I* need to be out there. I need to find him."

Sam nodded. It was obvious they needed to look for him.

But this wasn't simple.

It wasn't like he'd just wandered off.

Something had happened to him.

Something weird enough for him to have his clothes taken and wrapped around the dummy.

And he... Fuck.

He just worried about what he might find.

"We—we could be out there looking for him, and we're in here doing fucking nothing."

"We've got to think about how we're going to do things," Sam said. "Carefully."

Wayne frowned. Looked at Sam like he was going to punch the lights out of him. "What's there to think about, guv? My—my lad's out there. He's out there, and some fucking sick bastard's taken his clothes, and—"

"If you wouldn't mind toning down the language," Rebecca said. "You're—you're scaring my kid."

Wayne's face turned sour. "I'm sorry. I'm fucking sorry. Excuse me if I'm a little bit fucking tetchy right now. But—but my lad's gone missing. He's—he's gone missing, and we're all just standing talking, but we're not actually fucking *doing* anything."

"We need a plan," Sam said.

"A plan?"

"We can't all just go storming off into the woods. Firstly, because there's still children here. Including Millie. You don't... you don't want to go taking her towards whatever we're heading towards, do you?"

Wayne looked at Millie, and his face softened. He was back in the room again. And it was like he was realising Millie was still here. That there was another kid in his care, and he couldn't neglect her in trying to find Marky.

"Millie," he said. Crying. Shaking. "We'll—we'll find your brother. I'm sorry. I promise we'll find your brother."

She walked over to him and hugged him. And it was painful to witness. Painful, standing here in this dark kitchen and knowing what he knew.

That dummy.

The clothes.

And no sign of Marky.

No sign at all.

"We need to split into smaller groups. I'd rather we stuck together, but it is what it is. Wayne... Wayne and I should search the woods. But then that leaves Millie. So I'm... I'm not sure."

"I'm not standing in here while he's out there."

"And I get that. But you have to be comfortable with someone else watching Millie if that's the case. And how Millie feels about that."

Wayne looked at Millie.

She looked back up at him.

"One of—one of us could watch Millie and Leonard," Tristan said. His voice cracking a little bit.

Sam winced a bit when Tristan spoke. He seemed a decent enough bloke. But Sam felt allergic to him purely because he was Rebecca's fella now.

"One of you two watches the kids. The other and Tara... you go out and search the streets. See what you can find."

Tristan nodded. "I'll—I'd be okay with that."

"Bollocks," Rebecca said.

Tristan turned around. Frowning. "What?"

"I know you, Tristan. You're the biggest wuss going. *I'll* go out and search the streets with Tara. You'll stay here with the kids." And then she looked at Wayne. "He might be a wuss. But he's very good with children. You can trust him. Okay?"

Wayne nodded. And Sam knew it wasn't exactly ideal. Leaving his kid—the one kid he had left—with a bloke he'd barely met.

But Tristan did seem trustworthy, as much as it pained Sam to admit it.

He seemed a nice guy.

There was no ideal solution. But this was about the best they could put together.

"We head out. And if... if we have any trouble at all... we head straight back here, okay? Straight back here and into the cellar. Hide in there. But hopefully... hopefully, it won't come to that. But we have to be prepared."

Tara nodded.

He walked over to Wayne.

Looked right into his tear-stained eyes.

"Come on," Sam said. "Let's... let's go find your boy."

He could smell something too. Something sour. It smelled like bad food. He remembered when Mummy opened the fridge that time and all flies came buzzing out. The milk had gone off. And it smelled so bad. So bad it made Mummy sick.

That's what it smelled like right now.

So bad it was making him feel a bit sick, too.

But he wasn't sick.

He was strong.

He was going to be okay.

He felt something against his face. Something covering his eyes. So that's why it was dark. There was something in front of his eyes. Something stopping him from seeing.

He tried to reach up to move it away when he realised he couldn't move his hands.

They were tied behind his back.

So tight that his wrists were sore.

He started to panic a bit then because this wasn't a game.

And... and there was something else, too.

He was cold.

The clothes he was wearing. They didn't feel like his jeans or his Man United hoodie Wayne bought for him.

They felt... thinner.

Like pyjamas.

He didn't remember changing out his clothes.

When did that happen?

He tried to speak, and he realised something else.

His mouth was covered.

He couldn't say a word.

He sat there, and he felt a bit more nervous and a bit more scared.

Because he didn't know where he was.

All he remembered was...

Seeing that lady.

The nice lady with the smile.

Seeing her holding the torch and the toy.

Walking down the garden.

Ripping his jeans as he climbed through the bushes.

And then seeing the little cabin and walking over to it and...

It was all blurry after that.

But he remembered being carried somewhere.

He remembered waking up and someone stroking his hair and telling him it was all going to be okay.

Everything was going to be okay.

He shuffled on his chair and tried to move when he heard something in front of him.

Footsteps.

He froze.

Still.

Very still.

He sat there, and he listened.

No sounds now.

No sounds at all.

Except.

He could hear something.

Someone.

Breathing.

Breathing heavily, like he did when he had a cold.

He listened to them breathing, and he pictured a monster.

A horrible monster with spiky, scaly skin and brown goo dangling from its sharp teeth.

He sat there, and he felt a warm feeling on his leg, and he realised he was peeing, which embarrassed him because he couldn't let the monster see he was scared.

And then he heard footsteps.

Footsteps getting closer to him.

Step.

Step.

Step.

He heard those footsteps get closer until they stopped.

They stopped, right in front of him.

He sat there.

Crying underneath the thing covering his eyes.

The warmth on his leg getting stronger.

The smell of it getting worse, like when he wet the bed and went running to sleep with Mummy in the night—and sometimes he just did it so he had an excuse to sleep with them.

He sat there, totally still, and he waited for the monster to gobble him up and eat him.

And then he felt something strange.

A finger.

A cold finger stroking his cheek.

"Don't worry, my sweet boy," a voice said. A lady's voice. It sounded soft. It sounded nice. "None of my children have to worry about anything. Anything at all."

And then he felt her kiss him right in the middle of his head.

Smelled her breath, really bad, like rotten eggs.

Felt her fingers stroking his face softly.

Marky sat there, and he had no idea where he was.

He had no idea who this woman was.

And he had no idea how he'd got here.

But he wished he was back home.

He wished he hadn't stepped outside.

Because he was scared.

He was...

And then something happened that he didn't expect.

The lady pulled the blindfold away from his eyes.

And then he saw her.

Right in front of him.

Smiling.

CHAPTER ELEVEN

Marky opened his eyes.

It was dark all around. He wasn't scared. He felt calm. Relaxed. Like this was a game, and he knew everything was going to be okay.

But it was so dark. Darker than his bedroom ever got. Darker than *anywhere* ever got. Even when he turned out the lights and crawled under his bed and squeezed his eyes shut really right and pretended he was in space on the moon, it was even darker than that.

He could hear something. Something that sounded like water dripping. Mummy always told him and Millie to make sure they squeezed the tap tight after they'd done or the water would leak, and she'd end up paying the water people more money. Marky didn't really understand. Why did she have to pay money for water? And who were the water people? He imagined monsters. Mermaids with long, sharp teeth. He imagined fighting them and telling them to leave Mummy alone and then letting the tap run really, really fast just to annoy them. And then they could live happily ever after and never worry about water or the water people again.

"Hello, my child," she said. "You look tired. You should sleep some more."

And then she pressed a cloth to his nose, and at first, he was afraid, but then he was sleepy, then he was drifting, then he was in the clouds, and then he was...

Gone.

CHAPTER TWELVE

Sam had no idea how long he'd been inside the creepy old cabin searching every inch of it, but he wasn't having much luck.

It was dark in this cabin. There were so many cobwebs all over the place. Luckily, spiders didn't bother him. They always used to bother him as a kid. Used to freeze the second he saw one. Heart started racing. Throat seized up.

But as he got older, he grew more used to them. Forced himself to stand close to them. Then to pick them up. And in the end, it got to the point where he didn't mind leaving them in his bedroom, and then he got to a point where he didn't mind *catching* them and letting them free in his bedroom because at least he knew they were safe there.

Yeah. Weird, perhaps. But one way to conquer a phobia.

He could hear Wayne searching around the place. His footsteps against those creaky, rotting wooden floorboards. He could hear him muttering under his breath, too. Breathing heavily. He felt for him. He really did. The panic of losing this kid must be impossible to deal with. It was something Sam didn't expect he'd ever have to experience 'cause he never imagined he'd have kids.

But he didn't need to have kids to imagine what it might feel like to lose one.

The cabin smelled of damp and piss. The stench was so strong that Sam could taste it on his lips. So bad that it put him off eating altogether. It seemed like forever ago that he was cooking that can of chicken in sauce over a makeshift barbecue in the back yard of the house. It'd been burned and ruined at this point. A real waste of resources.

Harvey was here with them both, sniffing around. He didn't seem too fazed by events. Remarkably chilled, as ever. Perhaps *too* bloody chilled, sometimes.

Sam watched him sniffing around and hoped he might find some sort of lead. Some sign or some clue as to where Marky might've gone.

But he seemed more interested in the rusty old garden tools and the little cracks and crevices in the cabin than anything else. Smelled rats, probably.

Sam looked over at Wayne. He was outside now, squinting at the ground. Searching for footprints.

"Anything?" Sam asked.

Wayne looked around at him. Pale-faced. Haunted. A look that told him everything he needed to know.

Sam sighed. He didn't know what else to do. There were no clues in here, that was for sure.

Just that dummy.

That damned creepy dummy in the middle of the cabin.

He walked over to it.

Saw the clothes on it.

The jeans that had been fitted right over its legs.

The hoodie.

He looked down at that dummy as its eyes stared up at Sam, empty, vacant. It gave him the god-damned creeps.

"Wait," Wayne said.

Sam turned around. "Found something?"

Wayne didn't respond.

Sam stepped out of the cabin. Grateful to get out of the confines and back into the wooden area, even if it was grim out here, too.

Wayne was on his knees, squinting at something on the ground.

"What is it?" Sam asked.

"Do—do you see that?"

"I'm... not entirely sure what I'm looking at."

"Footprints," Wayne said.

Sam frowned. He definitely couldn't see anything on the ground. Especially not where Wayne was looking. "I..."

"Footprints," he said. "Look here. See."

Sam got a little closer.

Squinted at the ground.

He was about to tell Wayne he was imagining things when he saw them.

Prints.

Definite prints.

Hard to make out initially.

But once he saw them, they were hard to unseen.

He looked up. Followed those prints. They went off up ahead towards the thicker hedges and bushes. Somewhere in the distance, Sam heard shouting. It wasn't one of their people. It was on the street somewhere. A reminder that they weren't alone, even if they were in the middle of nowhere.

The second Sam noticed the prints, Wayne shot up.

He staggered forward, following their path.

"Wayne," Sam said.

"I've—I've got to find him."

"And I hear you," Sam said. "But we've got to be careful, too."

But Wayne wasn't hearing him.

He was racing along.

Following those prints.

Desperate to find Marky.

"Marky!" Wayne called. "It's—it's okay, Marky. I'm coming."

"Fucking hell," Sam said. He got it. Like, truly. It was bound to be impossible to think when your kid was missing—and when he was clearly in danger.

But...

They had to be careful.

'Cause they had no idea what they were running towards.

"Marky!" Wayne shouted. Still running along through the tall grass. Struggling to stay on his feet. "It's—it's okay. I'm coming. Don't worry. I'm coming."

He ran further, Sam following him and Harvey running alongside them both like this was all some big, fun game.

He kept on going until suddenly, he slipped over and fell face flat in the mud.

Right in the path of the prints.

"Shit," Wayne said. Dragging himself back to his feet. Covered in mud and water. "I... I lost it. I lost—I lost the trail."

Sam stood there and looked at Wayne as he spun around. Panicking. Lost. There was nothing about him that resembled the man Sam had first met. He was a completely changed man.

A scared man.

A broken man.

And as they stood there in the dark trenches of the woods, Sam didn't know what to do or what to say.

But looking at Wayne, he was drawn to doing one thing and one thing only.

He walked over to him.

He put a hand on his shoulder.

Squeezed it. Tight.

"Come on," Sam said. "It's okay. We'll find him. It's not over. Okay? Don't give up."

Wayne looked up at him. Tears filling his eyes. Rolling down his cheeks.

"It's not over. We're going to find him. It's going to be okay."

He saw Wayne nod.

Saw him open his mouth and go to say something.

And that's when he heard something.

Something right behind him.

Something in the trees and in the bushes.

An unmistakable sound.

A sound that sent shivers up Sam's spine.

Singing.

CHAPTER THIRTEEN

Tara wasn't sure how long she and Rebecca had been walking down the waterlogged road, but she was pretty sure about one thing.

They weren't finding Marky.

They were in the middle of nowhere, pretty much. The A6 was a busy road, but they were on a stretch of it just before Lancaster. Surrounded by fields on either side, which were usually filled with cows. The farmers had obviously taken them in, keeping them out of the way of the public eye. They would need their cattle now more than ever, especially if things kept deteriorating.

Which they would. Tara was sure of it.

There weren't even many cars abandoned on this stretch of road. It felt weird. Like they were in purgatory, somehow. She dreaded to think what the cities would be like now. She didn't want to have the misfortune of finding out.

She thought about the scenes she'd witnessed that first day.

And then the state of things a few days later, just outside the city centre.

The looting.

The fighting.

The desperation and the chaos.

The thought of being back in the midst of that made her feel ill.

And yet... what she'd give for *some* semblance of life right now.

Because this felt eerie.

The road was quiet. Every now and then, she called out Marky's name, and her voice echoed off into the distance for miles. She didn't want to draw any undue attention to herself, which was a weird feeling. She didn't have any supplies on her. And she wasn't in a dodgy area or an area where she would've felt remotely threatened before the power went out.

But it was just the thought of what Sam and Rebecca told her.

The thought of that dummy.

The thought of Marky's clothes dangling from its body.

The thought that something awful had happened to Marky.

That someone was out there.

She took a deep breath of the cool air. It smelled... damp. She was a little weary. Not surprising—she hadn't eaten properly for days. No appetite whatsoever. And the thought of food just made her sick.

She knew it wasn't good. She needed to eat, and she needed to keep her energy levels up.

But she knew she definitely wouldn't be eating today.

She looked around and saw Rebecca standing there, hands on her hips.

"What do you think?" Rebecca asked.

Rebecca was... nice. Annoyingly nice. And Tara knew it was weird to say "annoyingly nice" because it wasn't like she *wanted* her to be a bitch or anything, was it?

But she had to admit when she'd first met her that she was kind of rooting for her to be a bitch in a way that she couldn't totally explain.

She knew it probably had something to do with the fact she was developing feelings for Sam.

Which was something she still hadn't stared fully in the face, head-on, just yet.

Tara swallowed a lump in her throat. "I... I don't know how much longer we can just walk down the street shouting his name."

Rebecca nodded back. And then she shook her head. "If anything like this happened to Leonard... I don't know. I just... I feel so bad for Wayne. But I don't know... I don't know what else we can do."

Tara hated to admit it, but Rebecca was right. They'd been searching for ages now and with no luck.

And it was a horrible thing to face up to. You couldn't just give up looking for a lost child, could you?

But it wasn't like the old days.

They couldn't just put out a report to the police.

Marky was gone.

And unless they were very, very fortunate... the chances of them seeing him again were slim.

And growing slimmer by the moment.

"I just keep... I just keep thinking about how I'd feel," Rebecca said. "If it was my kid. And then... and then I keep thinking of him back in that house. And if anything happens to him while I'm away... I'd never forgive myself."

Tara nodded. "We've searched. I don't want to stop searching. Neither of us do."

"But it's feeling like we don't have much of a choice," Rebecca said.

"Right."

They both looked at each other. And Tara could see from the haunted look in Rebecca's eyes that she was coming to the same conclusion.

They were going to have to go back to the house.

They were going to have to give up.

They were going to have to break the awful news that they hadn't found anything.

Anything at all.

"Come on," Tara said. "We've... we've done what we can. For now. And... and it doesn't mean it's over. It doesn't mean we've lost him. We just... we just need to try something else."

Rebecca nodded back at her. "Right," she said.

But Tara knew what she'd said was just for her own conscience.

So they both felt more comfortable walking away from the task at hand.

But what else could they do?

What fucking else could they do?

She went to turn around and head back towards the derelict old house when she saw something in the fields up ahead that sent a shiver right down her spine.

Someone standing there.

Someone that looked like... a child.

Standing there.

Waving.

CHAPTER FOURTEEN

Sam heard the singing in the woods, and he froze.

It was a woman's voice. Soft. Beautiful, to be honest. Whoever was signing had a gorgeous voice. In another situation and another set of circumstances, he might even be able to appreciate it.

But right here, right now, right in the middle of the woods, searching for Marky after finding his clothes draped over a creepy-as-fuck ventriloquist's dummy... yeah, it definitely wasn't a sound he appreciated.

It freaked him the fuck out.

He looked around at Wayne. Saw him staring off towards that singing with wide eyes. Which meant it wasn't in Sam's imagination. Shit. He always clung to that hope whenever something freaked him out. He wasn't sure why. When had he ever hallucinated *anything* in his life?

The clouds had thickened overhead. The woods were dark. And other than that singing, everything was quiet. So damned quiet.

He could smell Wayne's sweat amidst the damp earth. He felt

dizzy, shaky, and a little weak, and he knew damned well he needed food in his system.

But the thought of eating anything right now made him feel sick.

That voice.

That woman singing in the woods.

He turned around slowly.

Looked for the source of that singing. For any signs of life. For any evidence that this *wasn't* the creepiest shit imaginable.

He didn't see anything.

He didn't see anyone.

But he could damn well *hear* where that singing was coming from.

He stood there—heart racing. The trees were thicker where the singing was coming from. The woods were darker over there, too. Of course they were. Of fucking *course* the singing was coming from the creepiest damned section of this overgrown woodland area.

He took a deep breath.

Because as much as he didn't want to find out who was singing, he knew he didn't have a choice.

Because chances were, whoever was singing had something to do with Marky's disappearance.

Or *everything* to do with Marky's disappearance.

Wayne started walking towards the singing. Fists tensed.

"Wait," Sam said.

Wayne looked around at him. Narrowed his eyes. "Why the fuck would I wait? That—that creep took my boy."

"We don't know that. Yet."

"Oh," Wayne said. "So there's just two fucking creeps hanging around in the woods? One of them's taken Marky, and the other just fancies practising her opera in the middle of a crisis? Really? Get fucking real, mate."

Sam had to admit Wayne had a point. What were the chances

of some other creep just hanging out here in the middle of these woods?

"Even so... we have to be careful."

"I'll be careful when I find my boy—"

"We don't know who they are or how many of them there are, and we don't know what they're capable of. So let's... let's just take this one step at a time. Okay? Let's just..."

And then Sam noticed something.

Wayne's eyes widened, too.

So he'd clearly noticed as well.

The singing.

It'd stopped.

He stood there. Heart pounding.

Looking right into Wayne's eyes as time stood still.

Wayne shook his head.

"I can't wait."

"Wayne."

"I can't..."

And then he turned around, and he ran.

Ran through the woods in the direction the singing came from.

Sam stood there and shook his head, Harvey by his side. "Jesus, Harv. What a fucking morning."

And then, as much as he didn't like it, as much as it felt like a terrible idea, he ran.

He ran through the woods after Wayne.

Wayne was well ahead. And Sam was losing sight of him.

Losing sight of him behind the branches.

Behind the trees.

"Marky!" Wayne shouted. His voice echoing through the silence. "What—what've you done with my Marky?"

And Sam knew any element of surprise or stealth element was gone now.

Whoever the singing woman was, she knew they were coming.

And if she had anything to do with Marky's disappearance, which seemed very fucking likely, then she would be long gone right now.

"Wayne!" Sam said. Realising there was no frigging point in even trying to be subtle anymore.

But Wayne wasn't turning around.

He kept on running.

And he was getting further and further ahead, further and further out of sight.

"Wayne," Sam said.

Wayne was out of sight now.

He was gone.

And at the pace he was going and the stitch fucking gnawing at Sam's chest, there was no catching up with him.

He planted his hands on his knees and took a deep breath through his nostrils when he saw something that filled him with fear.

Harvey.

He was still running.

Running on past Sam.

Running through that dark canopy of trees.

Running further into the darkness after Wayne.

"Harvey!" Sam shouted.

And he was usually good with recall. It was something Sam prided himself on. His successes training this dog.

But right now, he saw Harvey running off into the distance, off after Wayne, and he realised maybe he wasn't the dog whisperer after all.

"Harvey!" he shouted. His voice echoing through the woods.

He went to run after Harvey through the squelchy, muddy ground, when he heard something behind him.

Right behind him.

Something that filled him with terror.

Sam heard singing.

CHAPTER FIFTEEN

Tara saw the person she was convinced was a kid standing there in the middle of the field, waving, and she thought she must be seeing things.

God, she *hoped* she was seeing things.

Because this was creepy as fuck.

She stared across the field at that kid. A little boy, by the looks of things. He was just standing there, way in the distance, waving at her.

And he was too far away for Tara to tell whether it was Marky or not. He was kind of small. Dark hair. Hell, she wasn't even entirely sure if he was a child. Looked like one. But there was something... weird about it.

But... shit, she'd just pretty much described every frigging child around Marky's age on the planet, hadn't she? She'd hardly narrowed things down.

The streets were silent but for the breeze against the trees. The stench of the stagnant water filled her nostrils, making her feel a little queasy. She could taste copper on her lips. The taste of blood.

Jonno's blood.

Every time she thought of Jonno, she was right back there again.

Back in that cellar.

Jonno holding that rifle to her head.

Pushing it against her skull.

Hard.

And then she was squeezing her eyes and hearing the blast and—

"It's—it's him," Rebecca said.

Tara jumped. Rebecca's voice had jolted her back into the present moment.

The kid.

The kid, standing there in the middle of that field.

Waving.

"Are you sure?" Tara said.

Rebecca stared ahead. Wide-eyed. "It has to be him. Right?"

Tara squinted at that boy and wished she'd gone to the opticians *before* this catastrophe struck. That would've been really good timing, wouldn't it? Served her right for keeping on putting it off.

And then the boy lowered his hand.

He looked over his shoulder.

And then he ran away.

Fuck. No. That was *not* what Tara wanted to happen right now.

Because she knew what happened next.

She knew exactly what had to happen next.

She looked at Rebecca, and as much as she didn't want to admit it, a part of her wished she'd never seen the kid at all.

Because she knew she was going to have to chase him.

And the thought of chasing a kid who she wasn't even one-hundred percent certain *was* Marky across a field in the middle of bloody nowhere was definitely not at the top of her list of priorities right now.

But that kid was running away.

He was getting further and further away.

So Tara knew they didn't have a choice.

"Well," she said. "Here goes nothing."

They ran.

Clambered over the metal gate and landed in the boggy ground of the field. God, the cold water on her legs felt absolutely awful. It just felt like she was never going to get properly clean again. Or warm. Or dry. Every time she got close to either of those luxuries, naturally a boggy field would appear right in front of her just to ruin her fucking day.

She ran through the thick mud of the field as quick as she could. But it wasn't easy. The ground was sinking. The mud was getting thicker. And before she knew it, she had mud and water up to her knees.

"Has anyone ever drowned in a field before?" Rebecca asked. Struggling her way across the mud bath just as much as Tara.

Tara dragged her right leg up and out of the mud and into another patch. Fuck. It felt like it was getting deeper with every step. "I think—I think we're about to find out."

She looked up over to where the kid stood waving.

He was gone now.

Out of sight.

Nowhere to be seen.

She stood there, and she scanned the fields. There was a farm up ahead. Maybe he'd run over there. Maybe he'd gone wandering in the night and got lost and found this farm. Maybe he was waving because he'd seen them, and now he was just playing an innocent game of hide and seek.

It was a viable explanation.

Right?

She went to drag her right leg out of the mud and continue her journey across this literal mud bath when she realised something horrifying.

Her right leg.

It was stuck.

She tried to pull it out. Shifted her weight onto her left leg to get more leverage.

But she was stuck.

Her right leg was stuck.

And her left leg was sinking further down.

She was sinking further down.

Rebecca continued traipsing through the mud, making it look easy.

And Tara tried dragging her right leg out.

Then tried dragging her left leg out.

But it was no use.

It was no fucking use either way.

She was stuck.

Stuck in the fucking mud.

She stood there, really still. 'Cause struggling wasn't helping her at all.

And she could feel herself sinking.

Feel the mud mid-way up her thighs now.

The cold water beneath seeping through her jeans.

Rebecca turned round. "Tara?"

And Tara saw the concern in her eyes. Which fucking *concerned* her even more.

Because if someone else looked worried, that almost definitely meant you were completely and utterly screwed.

"I—I'm okay. I just..."

She didn't want to ask for help.

Desperately didn't want to make a tit of herself in front of Sam's ex-wife.

Didn't want someone else to be responsible for her once again.

She wanted to be *strong*.

She felt herself sinking further. Felt the mud and the water right up to her hips now.

Rebecca staggered over to her.

"It's alright," she said. "I'll—I'll give you a hand."

But Tara kept on straining to get out.

Straining to free herself.

Eager to get out of here without anyone else's help.

Rebecca leaned forward at full stretch. "Grab my hand."

Tara put her hands against the muddy ground, which was barely even "ground" anymore. It was just water. Water and mud.

"Tara!" Rebecca said. "Grab my hand."

Tara looked up into Rebecca's eyes, and as much as she didn't want to be that damsel in distress, once a-fucking-gain, she knew this was life and death right now.

She gritted her teeth.

And then she grabbed Rebecca's hand.

And for a moment, just a moment, as Rebecca's warm hand held on to hers and started pulling her up and out of the mud, she felt safe.

She felt like she'd dodged a bullet.

Like she was going to be okay.

And then Rebecca slipped.

She slipped and fell back.

Tumbled down into the mud herself.

Landed on her back.

Scrambled around and tried to get back to her feet.

"I'm—I'm stuck," she said. "I can't... I can't..."

And as Tara stood there, the mud up to her waist, she looked into Rebecca's eyes as she struggled to break free of the sinking mud, and in the loneliness of this vast, empty, open field, she had a horrifying realisation.

She was going to sink under the mud.

She was going to drown here.

They were both going to die here.

CHAPTER SIXTEEN

Singing.

Singing behind Sam.

Right bloody behind Sam.

He stared ahead at that dark section of woods up ahead. He'd watched Wayne disappear through there. And he'd watched Harvey disappear through there after him, too.

He wanted to get to Wayne.

And more importantly, he wanted to get to Harvey.

He didn't want to let him get any further away.

He didn't want to lose him.

But that singing.

That singing, right behind him.

Those footsteps, right behind him.

And that unshakeable feeling that there was someone watching him.

Staring right at him.

As much as he wanted to keep on running... he needed to look over his shoulder.

He needed to see.

He could smell something in the air. Something... sweet. Like perfume. Too much perfume, tickling his nostrils, getting on his chest. So strong he could taste it, like the contents of an inhaler.

And that singing.

That heavenly singing sending shivers down his spine.

He stood there, rooted to the spot.

Unable to turn around.

Unable to move.

But knowing damned well he had to.

He took a deep breath, and he went to turn around when he noticed something.

Again, the singing had stopped.

And this time...

This time, he could hear footsteps.

Footsteps walking across the muddy, slushy woodland floor.

Walking closer towards him.

He tightened his fists.

Turned around.

Slowly.

He had to face this woman.

And he had to be ready.

He turned around, looking over his shoulder when he saw her standing right there, in the corner of his eye.

She was close.

So close.

Literally a few inches away from him.

He could hear her breathing heavily, croakily.

And it sounded like she was mumbling things.

Muttering things under her breath.

He turned around even more so he was facing her head-on.

It was an old woman. Her skin was cracked and leathery. She was gaunt and frail. She was wearing a dirty white nighty. Her eyes looked glazed over like she had cataracts or like she was blind.

She was holding on to a piece of tissue paper, which she kept on turning around in her hand. Rolling between her fingers. Tearing chunks from.

And she was looking right at Sam.

Smiling.

Seeing her... seeing her gave Sam the creeps even more. Because now he *definitely* knew for certain he wasn't imagining things. Now he knew for definite that she was here, and she was real and standing right bloody opposite him.

But at the same time, he didn't feel quite as scared.

Because she didn't look like the sort of woman who'd abduct a kid.

She didn't look physically capable of anything like that.

Or mentally capable.

She looked like a lost old lady.

"Are you—are you okay?" Sam asked.

The woman tilted her head. Her baggy eyelids narrowed, and she squinted right at him. Like he was trying to find him. Trying to see him.

And he wondered if she could even see him.

If she could even hear him.

She was old. So old. And it wouldn't surprise him if she was deaf as well as blind.

She stood right there, squinting, reeking of perfume, when suddenly she opened her mouth, and she stared singing again.

The hairs on Sam's arms stood right on end. She was good. Really good. She had a beautiful voice. And if this wasn't as urgent a fucking situation as it was right now, he might've been able to enjoy it.

There was something sad to this whole thing.

This ancient woman, out here in the woods, completely alone.

This old lady lost in the woods.

Singing.

He went to look over his shoulder in the direction Wayne and Harvey had disappeared.

There was still no sign of them.

And then he looked back round, and he noticed something.

This woman.

He recognised her.

The photos. The photos in the house.

The photos might be old, many in black and white.

But he recognised her.

It was the woman from those photos.

He looked at her now, standing here with that long, thin hair, and he felt even more sorry for her.

This woman was *living* in that derelict old house?

Fuck. That was rough. Even before the blackout, that was rough.

He looked at her, and he felt sorry for her.

So old.

So frail.

So weak.

And as much as he knew he had to go find Wayne and Harvey and tell Wayne about what he'd found—tell them the singing had nothing to do with the kidnapping—he needed to get this woman back to her home, too.

She stared at him.

Stared right at him with those empty, vacant eyes.

"Have you seen my cat?" she muttered. "Mr Tibbles is—is usually home by now. I'm worried he might've got caught in the explosions. I—I heard the alarm. Tried to find the air raid shelter. But I... I just can't find it?"

He saw her looking around. Shaking a little. Tearing that tissue paper even harder.

"Don't worry," Sam said. "The... the bombs didn't hit. And I'm sure... I'm sure Mr Tibbles is back home waiting for you."

"You think?" she asked.

Sam nodded. And he felt so sorry for this woman. He'd seen his grandma fall victim to dementia. It was horrible to witness. A woman so funny, a woman so proud. First, the memory loss. Forgetting simple things like what she'd gone to the supermarket for or where she'd left her car keys.

And then, when she lost her car, she'd still go out, searching for it. End up walking miles, only to be found passed out on a park bench by a passer-by.

In the end, she lost her ability to speak. Shit the bed all time and spoiled the carpets. It was so sad, seeing a woman so proud sink to those depths. The Grandma he knew and loved would hate for other people to see her in that way.

So when she finally passed away, it was a blessing, in a sense.

Because Grandma had died years before. The Grandma they all knew, anyway.

She wouldn't have wanted the people she cared about seeing her like that.

He looked at this woman now, and as much as he knew he needed to find Wayne, Harvey, and fucking Marky, too... he saw Grandma in this woman.

And he wanted to make her comfortable.

He wanted to take her back home.

He went to link her arm when she looked right into his eyes.

And there was something different in those eyes now.

There was a look of fear.

"Will they be there?" she asked.

Sam frowned. "Will *who* be there?"

She looked at him with total lucidity.

"The—the others," she said. "The ones who... the ones who stay there."

He heard her panic and saw the fear in her eyes, and he felt a shiver down his spine.

The others?

Who were the others she was so worried about?

Did they have something to do with Marky?

He went to ask her who she was talking about when suddenly he heard something right behind him.

Footsteps.

"Oh no," the woman said, staring off over Sam's shoulder now. "They're—they're here. The others. They're here already."

CHAPTER SEVENTEEN

Tara always thought she'd die a really exciting death.

She always imagined she'd be one of the victims of a plane crash. Because it didn't matter that the odds were slim—telling someone hurtling towards the earth at God knows how many miles per hour that the odds of dying in a plane accident were slim didn't really change a fucking thing to them, did it?

Or something else. Struck by lightning, maybe. She remembered going for a walk with Jonno not long after she'd first met him. Forgetting to lock the door, so quickly nipping back before beginning that walk, hand in hand. Not long after they'd set off, a lightning bolt appeared out of nowhere, blasting a tree just metres in front of her and Jonno. The top of the tree tumbled down to the ground, landing with an immense crack.

And as Tara stood there, she wondered what would've happened if she'd remembered to lock the door after all.

Would she even be alive today?

But there was one way Tara definitely never expected to die.

And that was death by drowning in a fucking farmer's field.

The skies were a beautiful deathly shade of grey. Of course, they fucking were. What other colour were they going to be when she was facing near certain death? Pathetic fallacy exists, bitches, and it's ready and waiting for you to be drowning in a fucking field with no hope of getting the fuck out.

She was covered in mud and water right up to her neck now. She was cold. So fucking cold. Slimy mud covered her body. Icy water dragged her down to the depths below. She could taste shit. Cow shit and manure. The farmers had been muck spreading pretty recently. Fuck. What a way to die. Drowning in shit.

And the worst thing?

Every time she tried to move, she felt herself sinking further down to the depths below.

Every time she struggled and scrambled for some leverage, she sunk further down.

So she stayed as still as she could. As still as she possibly fucking could.

Slowly drifting down.

Slowly, slowly...

"Tara!"

Rebecca. Fuck. She sounded in danger. In big danger. Sounded like she was spluttering some of the mud and water.

And Tara wanted to reassure her. Hell, she wanted to *help* her.

But she couldn't even reassure herself right now.

She couldn't help herself.

"I want—I want to say it's going to be okay," Tara said. "But I... I don't know. I just don't—"

Rancid, dirty water filled her mouth.

Tickled her throat.

Made her cough and splutter.

And instinctively, she lashed around.

Reached out for something to hold on to.

And sunk down even more as she did.

She sunk so deep now that the water was covering her mouth.

It was covering her mouth, and it was tickling her nostrils with its awful shitty smell.

And as she hung there in stasis, unable to actually believe this was happening to her as the horror took over her, she thought back to her childhood again.

She was there again.

Standing by the side of that pond.

Standing there and holding her down and watching the bubbles seep out of her lips and—

No!

She struggled a little more.

Struggled until the water tickled her nostrils even more.

Until it started seeping up there.

Seeping up and creeping up into them and—

No.

Hold on.

Hold on...

She squeezed her eyes shut, and as much as she didn't want to be a whining bitch, she felt herself crying. And she felt pathetic. So pathetic.

All these years of telling herself she was strong.

All these years of telling herself she could make it on her own, here she was.

Drowning.

Drowning in a mud bath.

It was typical.

It was just fucking typical, wasn't it?

She opened her stinging eyes as the water covered her nostrils. Tried to stretch up so she could get some air, but she couldn't. The moment had gone. The moment had passed.

She looked up. Lifted her head and tilted it back just to get a little more air.

And she saw those eyes.

Saw them staring down at her.

Saw them staring down at her just like they'd stared up at her from that pond.

Those eyes.

Those bloodshot, desperate eyes.

Tara squeezed her eyes shut.

Forced herself to forget.

Forced herself to forget as the dirty water covered her face.

As the muddy arms beneath her dragged her down.

And as darkness surrounded her.

She kept her eyes squeezed shut. The water was filthy, and she didn't want it to get in her eyes. Which was fucking ridiculous, wasn't it? She was dying here. She was going to drown, and she was worrying about a bit of shit in her eye?

She held her breath. Heart racing harder. The darkness surrounding her more and more.

She felt herself sinking further and further.

And there was nothing she could do.

She tried to grab the chunks of mud around her, but they just crumbled away.

She tried to stretch herself up towards the surface, desperate for a breath of air, but the more she tried, the further away it grew.

She struggled, scrambled, and tried to climb her way up and out of this cesspit.

But the more she struggled, the more she sank.

She couldn't hold her breath anymore.

She couldn't keep her eyes shut anymore.

She opened her eyes.

Saw nothing but darkness above.

Darkness, and the eyes of *him*.

The eyes of the boy in the pond.

The eyes of...

She felt her vision fading.

She felt the water around her warming up, cocooning her, whispering that it was okay to open her mouth, that it was okay to breathe, while her brain screamed at her not to.

She felt herself drifting.

Felt herself sinking.

She felt herself falling.

And then, when she felt that warmth close around her... Tara felt no fear.

She took a deep breath, opened her mouth, and she let the murky water in.

CHAPTER EIGHTEEN

"It's the others. They're—they're here already. Oh gosh, they're here already."

Sam heard the fear in this poor old woman's voice, and he had to admit he felt pretty fucking afraid himself now.

They were right bang in the middle of this overgrown woodland area behind this woman's house. It was dark in here, now the sun had disappeared behind the clouds. He swore the wind was picking up, too, bringing a chill to the air. He wanted to get out of here. Get out of these woods.

But at the same time, he knew he couldn't walk away.

'Cause Harvey was missing.

And Wayne was missing.

He had to find them before he got out of here.

And then there was Marky.

And now...

Now, he could hear footsteps behind him.

The footsteps of those this woman called the "others."

Which was really fucking creepy.

He heard them getting closer. Squelching through the mud.

He saw the look of horror on that woman's face. Her misty eyes widening every second.

Whoever these "others" were, they didn't strike Sam as people he really wanted to run into any time soon.

He stood there. Heart thudding. He was fucking knackered, to be honest. He really wasn't in the mood for another fight right now.

"Please—please just don't let them back to my house. Please... Not... not them."

Sam gulped.

"Don't worry, love," he said. "I'll take care of them."

He turned around and cracked his knuckles when he saw someone he didn't expect.

It was Wayne.

Wayne was standing there.

Staring at Sam.

Wide-eyed.

"Wayne?" Sam asked.

"What's—what's going on here?"

"This is... She owns the house. The one we're staying in."

"What does she know about Marky?" he said, marching closer towards her.

"Hey," Sam said, lifting a hand. "Back off, okay? She doesn't know anything about Marky."

"Please," the old lady said, covering her ears. "Make—make it go away. Make it stop."

"What have you done with Marky?"

"She's—she's got dementia, okay?" Sam said, holding up a hand and stopping Wayne getting any closer. "She's—she's nothing to do with Marky."

"And you know that for sure, do you?"

"I'm as sure as I can be."

Wayne looked over Sam's shoulder, over at that woman.

"You seen any kid come running through here?"

The woman covered her ears. Squeezed her eyes shut. And she shook violently. She looked freezing. She must've been out here all night. Poor woman.

"We need to get her back to her home," Sam said.

"We need to find Marky."

"I know. Harvey. He... he came after you too."

Wayne shrugged. "Didn't see him."

Fuck. So Harvey was missing now, too.

Harvey was missing, and Marky was missing, and this woman really needed to get back home 'cause she wasn't safe out here.

"Look," Wayne said. "You take her back. I'll keep looking for Marky. And I'll look for Harvey, too. Doesn't make sense for the pair of us to be out here anymore. Besides. She needs help like you said."

Sam nodded. "I appreciate that. I'll be back out here the second I'm done, I swear."

Wayne nodded again. "Check on Millie while you're back. She's a good kid. This... all this. It's not easy on her."

Sam nodded again. "I will do."

"And Sam?"

"What?"

"Thanks. For... for helping. I know... I know I ain't been the best."

"You mean before you stabbed me in the leg or since then?"

"Both. I just... My boy's out there. I promised Carly. I promised her I'd look after them, that I'd protect them both. No matter what. If anything's happened to him... I can't live with myself."

"You'll find him," Sam said. "And you *will* live for yourself. Because Millie's back home. And you have to be strong for her, too, remember?"

Wayne took a deep breath. Rubbed his hands through his hair. "Thanks," he said.

He looked into Sam's eyes.

"I'll look for your dog. I'll get him back. Think the kids quite like him, too."

"He's a good dog," Sam said.

He stood there, time standing still.

"Good luck," Sam said.

"Yeah," he said. "You too."

And then Wayne turned around and walked away again and into the woods.

Sam watched Wayne disappear.

He watched him vanish, further and further away, deeper into the trees.

He hoped he was going to be okay.

He hoped he'd see him again soon.

"Come on," he said to the old woman, linking her arm. "Let's get you back home."

He looked back at where Wayne had disappeared, over to the trees.

And as much as he didn't want to admit it, he had a horrible feeling he would never see Wayne again.

He didn't know it yet, but he wasn't too far off the mark.

CHAPTER NINETEEN

Wayne saw the movement in the trees and felt a shiver down his spine.

Because for a moment, for just a moment, he asked himself the question.

What if it wasn't Marky?

What if it wasn't Harvey?

What if it was someone else?

The woods were thick. Dark. He couldn't see much, mostly because the sky above was grey, too. He felt cold. Shivery. He didn't know how much of that was the adrenaline, the shock, the horror of everything he was going through, and how much of it was the coldness of these woods themselves.

He just kept thinking of what Sam said.

That woman.

The old woman standing there in the middle of the woods.

The way she was singing.

Signing so fucking beautifully but so fucking creepily.

He thought back to what Sam said about her. About how she didn't have a clue about Marky. Didn't have a clue about anything.

And even though he couldn't help but agree with him based on all he'd seen... he still had that question on his mind.

What if she was lying?

What if she wasn't all she seemed?

What if there was summat else going on here?

And who the hell were these "others" she kept talking about?

He squinted ahead into the dark. Looked at the thicker hedges up ahead. Something was moving around in there. Something twitching in there. Something kept catching his eye in there.

And he didn't know what it was. He wanted to believe it was Marky. That he'd just done a runner or got lost in the night, but he was okay now. 'Cause Wayne couldn't live with the thought that summat might've happened to him. That he might be in danger.

It was quiet in these woods. Quiet, but for the branches scraping against each other in the wind. The smell of damp was strong in the air. His toes felt freezing cold. Freezing from the water seeping through the cracks in his trainers.

He kept on thinking of Millie back home. God, he felt so fucking bad for leaving her there with people she barely knew. What if summat happened to her, too, when he wasn't looking? While he was absent, again?

He thought about her.

Sam was decent. A good bloke. He felt kind of guilty about slashing his leg the other day. But he'd been pretty desperate. He hoped Sam had forgiven him at this point.

He hoped he'd go back and he'd look after Millie.

He saw that shuffling in the trees up ahead. The hairs on the back of his neck stood on end. He kind of didn't want to say anything 'cause he didn't want to draw any attention to himself. But at the same time... if it was Marky or Harvey, then maybe that's exactly what he needed to do. Speak. Say summat. Make them feel more comfortable. Make them feel okay.

He cleared his throat. "Marky?"

No response.

The bushes kept on shuffling.

He took another deep breath.

Crept closer.

"Marky," he said. "If it's—if it's you, buddy, it's me. It's—it's Wayne. It's gonna be alright."

He walked closer. Inched ever closer.

But the closer he got, the more his nerves grew.

The more anxious he grew.

Because if it were Marky... he'd've said summat back at this point.

He'd definitely have said something at this point.

He inched further towards the shuffling when he noticed something.

The movement.

It'd stopped.

But he could hear more movement.

More movement, over to the left.

He froze.

Stood still.

Very fucking still.

He turned his head.

Slowly.

He could see something.

Something there in the woods.

Something like... eyes.

He felt a shiver down his spine.

Turned around even further and faced those eyes head-on.

"Marky?" he said. There was someone there, for sure. Watching him.

But he couldn't tell whether it was a person.

Or a dog.

Or... anything else.

He walked towards those eyes slowly.

The closer he got to them, the less clear they became.

"It's okay," Wayne said. "Whoever... whoever it is, it's okay. Everything's gonna be okay."

He got closer to the eyes.

Right to the bush before them.

He stood there.

Stopped.

Heart racing.

What if it wasn't who he thought it was?

What if it wasn't Marky *or* Harvey?

Fuck.

There was only one way to find out.

He grabbed the outside of the bush, ready to pull it apart.

And then he heard growling.

Right behind him.

Growling.

Growling that sent the hairs on the back of his neck standing right on end.

He turned around slowly, getting ready to face whatever it was he was about to face, when he saw it.

A dog.

Standing right there.

Staring at him.

"Harvey," he said.

Harvey wagged his tail a little when Wayne said his name.

And then he started growling again.

Growling and staring right at Wayne.

"It's alright," Wayne said. "It's—it's me. We've met, pal. You know who I am. You know..."

And then it struck Wayne.

The eyes.

The eyes in the bush.

The movement.

There was someone else here.

Someone right behind him.

Someone Harvey was growling at.

He went to spin around when suddenly he felt something crack him over the side of the head, hard.

He heard ringing in his ears.

Tasted blood.

And as he fell to the cold, damp ground, he saw a figure standing over him.

Crowbar in hand.

"Ssh," the figure said. "You don't need to worry anymore. You're going to be just..."

And then his consciousness drifted, and there was nothing but darkness.

CHAPTER TWENTY

Sam held the old woman's arm and walked back towards the house, and he couldn't shake that eerie feeling that someone was watching.

The skies had gone grey again. Looked rainy. Like the heavens might just open the hell up all over again, drowning the country in a way it most definitely couldn't handle anymore of. There'd been more than enough rain in the early days of the blackout. And while that rain had eased lately, the ground was still damp, and the roads were still flooded.

Any more rain and Sam wasn't sure it would ever drain away.

He looked over his shoulder, back into the woods. He thought about Wayne, and he thought about Harvey and Marky. He didn't want to give up the search for either of them. But he had to trust Wayne. They had an agreement. They had a deal. And part of Sam's side of the deal was that he got back to the house, got this woman back home, and ensured Millie and the others were okay back at the house.

He thought about going back into the woods. Finding Wayne. Because... because he didn't know. He had a weird fucking feeling about this. A *bad* fucking feeling about it.

But then he felt the old woman's cold, frail arm, and he knew he needed to get her back home. He couldn't leave her out here much longer.

"I—I'm worried," she said.

"You don't have to worry anymore," Sam said, taking a deep breath of the cool, fresh air.

"But—but the others."

"It's okay," Sam said. "That man you saw before. And the dog. They... they're my... they're my friends. We don't mean you no harm. We just... We kept an eye on your house last night. Made sure everything was okay. And it was. It really was. So you don't have to worry about anything anymore."

But the woman looked bothered. She kept on scratching at her arms. Looking over her shoulder, back towards the house.

"Trust me," Sam said. "Everything's going to be okay. I promise."

The woman didn't seem convinced. But she was at least partly comforted by Sam's words.

He looked at her. She was old. So old and so frail. She could barely put one foot in front of the other. Her skin was blue and grey. She looked dirty. So dirty. He had no idea how she'd got out of here. How she'd made it this far. He just hoped she was gonna be okay. He didn't want to have to worry about summat else.

As he held her arm, it reminded him of his old nan. She was a good woman. A woman he loved. He used to love the walks through the woods with her. Holding her hand. Crunching through the autumn leaves. He almost felt like he was back there now. Wrapped up in his warm fleecy parka. Cold air against his rosy cheeks. His nan laughing and joking beside him about something.

He held on to the woman's arm.

"What's your name?" he asked.

The woman muttered a couple of things under her breath. Things it was hard to make sense of.

"I'm... I'm Sam."

The old woman said nothing.

"I... I know how scared you must be. But... but I promise you've got nothing to worry about. Not with us."

"I'm Lydia," she said.

"Lydia," Sam said. "Lovely name."

Lydia looked at him, and a little warm smile crept across her face. "You flatter me."

"No, really. I like it."

"Maybe you are alright after all," Lydia said.

"I hope so," Sam said.

They walked further through the woods. And then Sam saw Lydia's old house right there, up ahead.

"What you doing out here in the woods anyway?"

"I don't... I don't like it when the others are there."

Sam narrowed his eyes. She must've seem him and his people coming. Must've spooked her. Poor woman.

"You don't have to worry about us. Like I said. You can trust me. And my friends."

Lydia looked over her shoulder, then back ahead. "Hmm."

"We're... we're going to get you back home. And once you're there, you're going to feel a lot better about everything—"

"But I won't," Lydia snapped. Her mood suddenly turning. Her eyes widening. The fear there to see. "Because—because *they'll* be there. The ones—the ones who come. The others."

Sam narrowed his eyes even more. Lydia wasn't making sense.

But then he had a thought.

What if she *was* making sense?

What if she was making complete sense, and he was just refusing to see it right in front of him?

He looked around at the house. He could see the windows now. The condensation, dust-covered windows.

"I don't—I don't want to see them again," Lydia said.

A shiver crept up Sam's spine.

"They—they bully me," she said. "Don't—don't take me back there. Please."

And as Sam stood there, it made sense.

It suddenly made total sense.

Someone was standing there in the bedroom window.

And it wasn't someone Sam recognised.

It was someone else.

The others.

CHAPTER TWENTY-ONE

Tom Pennance stood at the bedroom window and saw his old step mum out there with that bloke, and for the first time in years, he sensed trouble.

It was grey outside. At least it wasn't pissing it down anymore. When it was pissing down, a lot of people walked past this place looking for shelter. They were losing their shit now the power had gone out. Acting like it was the end of the frigging world.

Tom knew what it was like to live without power.

He knew too well.

He saw them walking through the garden. Saw that bloke linking Lydia's arm. He looked pretty tough. Pretty well-built. He'd been watching him for a little bit now. He'd been up in the attic all night, hiding away and out of sight.

'Cause it was important to figure out how tough they were.

It was important to figure out whether they had owt of value to them.

And it was important to figure out if they had anything they could take from them.

Anything they could offer them.

Or if they were a threat.

But as Tom stood here now and looked outside... he was beginning to think maybe these people might be a problem after all.

'Cause this bloke looked tough.

He looked like he *cared*.

And that was a problem.

He watched them get further and further across the garden. Saw them talking to one another. Saw Lydia *smiling*.

And he didn't like that.

He didn't like that shit at all.

She didn't *deserve* to smile.

Not after she'd stolen everything from him.

Everything that should've been his when Dad died went right to her.

He knew he could probably take her out without a problem. But it made more sense to keep her alive.

'Cause she was loaded.

She was loaded, and she could support his life.

Only... now, the power was gone.

Now, all access to her money was gone.

Now, she was losing her worth.

He knew he was mean to her sometimes. He knew he didn't always treat her good. But she wasn't good to him when he was younger, either.

So she deserved it.

She had it coming.

Only now...

He knew these people were gonna be a problem.

He saw the man look up towards him.

Saw him look right into his eyes.

Locked eyes with him, just for a second.

His stomach sank.

Because he knew what that meant.

He could see that weird look of recognition on this bloke's

face as if he was putting two and two together.

As if he understood something.

He gulped.

"It's time, folks," he said.

Shuffling behind him.

Wardrobe doors opening.

The smell of weed creeping closer.

And then, around him, he saw them appear.

All of them standing there beside him.

His friends.

His people.

"What do we do?" Shel asked.

Tom tightened his fists.

"One thing's for sure," Tom said. "We're not losing this place. No matter what. Because this is *my* home. And we're gonna defend it. No matter what."

CHAPTER TWENTY-TWO

Tristan wasn't sure how long he'd been in the house looking after these two kids on his own when he suddenly heard the footsteps upstairs.

It was dark and gloomy in this house. It really was not pleasant. He wasn't used to squalid conditions like this. He'd always been pretty fortunate. Grew up in wealth. Went to university and got a good degree in Biomedicine and then went right into something completely different—his dad's finance company. He didn't really need the degree, in all truth. He figured it was just his dad's way of making him prove that he was a hard worker. That he was competent. Capable.

And he'd proven that. Gone on to live a relatively carefree life. Met the woman he thought was the love of his life, Tabby, at twenty-one. Lost her to a car accident a few years later.

And those were awful years. They were horrible years. They were challenging years. Challenging beyond measure.

He'd contemplated ending it all multiple times. Because he was in his thirties, and it didn't feel like life was getting any better. It felt like he'd peaked, and it would only get worse. That it was only going one direction, and that was a very rapid downhill.

And then, when he'd been at his lowest, he'd met Rebecca, and everything changed.

Rebecca was lovely from the moment he met her. She'd had a marriage of her own deteriorate. She awoke something in him. Illuminated something. She made him want to live again.

And when he met Rebecca... even though she was different to Tabby, even though he loved her differently to the way he loved Tabby... she made him realise there was still so much to live for. So, so much.

He'd had a kid with her. Little Leonard. And he was here right now. Here in front of him, playing some board game with Millie, Wayne's kid.

And he was so good, was Leonard. So, so good.

He dreaded to think of his mum out there.

Of something happening to her.

He thought about the bloke, too. Sam. He'd heard a lot about Sam. How they'd had a really good marriage, only it went down-hill and collapsed when he suffered from a bout of serious depression or something.

She spoke fondly of him. Not in a way that made Tristan jealous or envious or concerned in any way at all.

But she spoke of the good man he was.

And now... now he was here, it was weird.

He wasn't a jealous man. Wasn't a bitter man at all.

But it was still an absurd, unusual situation to be in.

It didn't feel normal.

He was just going to have to take a breath and take it on the chin.

And then he heard the footsteps.

Upstairs.

He looked up at the dusty, dirty ceiling. Was it the wind?

No. Definitely not the wind.

Footsteps.

Definitely footsteps.

He looked down at Leonard and Millie. He didn't want to leave them. Didn't want to let them out of his sight.

But what if Marky was up there?

They'd searched the house.

But what if he was somewhere in here all along?

He looked at the kids. He wanted to take them with him.

But at the same time... he didn't want to take them with him.

'Cause what if there was someone up there who *wasn't* Marky?

What if it was someone dangerous?

"Kids," Tristan said.

Millie and Leonard both looked up at him, clearly not happy about being disturbed from their game.

"If—if I go upstairs just to check something, will you promise me you won't move a muscle?'

"Why do you need to go upstairs?" Millie asked.

"I just... I just do, okay? You'll keep an eye on Leonard for me, won't you?"

Millie nodded. "Course."

Tristan stood up. Barely able to believe he was actually doing this.

He stopped right at the door.

"And if... if you hear anything or see anything or anyone, you shout for me, okay? You shout at the top of your lungs."

"Where are you going, Daddy?" Leonard asked.

Tristan stood there. His heart felt like it sank right into his stomach.

He gritted his teeth and took a deep breath.

"Don't worry," he said. "You and Millie play nicely. And I'll be back in no time at all."

He looked into Leonard's eyes.

Smiled at him.

And then he turned around.

Walked out of the lounge.

Into the dingy hallway.

He walked to the bottom of the stairs and looked up there.

Silence.

"Marky?" he called. His voice echoing up the staircase.

No response.

He climbed up the creaky steps slowly. Every single step, he swore he heard something above him. Like there was someone up there.

But the further he got, the more he realised it was just his own footsteps.

It was just his own feet creaking against the floorboards.

He kept his fists clenched tight.

Got further up to the top.

And then he heard something else.

The attic.

The attic, which had these metal spiral stairs leading up towards it.

He heard movement up there.

He looked back down the stairs, heart racing.

Maybe he could just stay here.

Maybe he could just watch.

Maybe he could just wait.

He didn't want to disturb the wasp's nest if that's what was waiting up there for him.

But at the same time...

He gulped.

Walked up the last of the stairs.

Walked up towards that spiral staircase.

Looked up into the dusty darkness.

And then he cleared his throat.

"It's okay," he muttered to himself. "Just... just taking a look. That's all."

He climbed up the steps.

Heard his feet echoing against the metal.

Heard that metal creaking the further he climbed.

He climbed further and further up those stairs. He couldn't hear anything up there. Not anymore.

Maybe it was just the wind.

Maybe he was just imagining things.

He got higher up those stairs and peeked his head inside the loft room.

He didn't see anything.

Boxes.

Ancient wardrobes.

And...

Tristan's skin went cold.

By the window, he saw the outline of a woman.

Definitely not Marky, that was for sure.

Not anyone Tristan recognised.

"What..." he started.

And before he had the chance to even *begin* to understand, he felt a hand grab his ankle and drag him down the stairs.

Cracked his head against one of those metal steps.

Tasted blood.

And before he could call out to the kids to warn them, a hand covered his mouth.

He looked up.

Saw a man staring down at him.

Pale.

Bearded.

Skin covered in sores.

Smiling.

"Not so fast," the man said.

CHAPTER TWENTY-THREE

Tara opened her eyes.

She wasn't submerged in a pit of dirty water. Which was progress, to say the fucking least. She felt... warm, weirdly. Definitely an odd feeling. She hadn't felt truly warm for days now.

Was the whole blackout thing just a nightmare?

Had she imagined it all?

Maybe it was her mind's weird way of "escaping" the horrors of her relationship with Jonno. If so, it'd picked a weird fucking hallucination to project for her.

But no. She was pretty sure all that shit was real. She was mostly just surprised and a little amazed that she was still alive right now.

Unless she wasn't alive. Maybe this was what heaven felt like.

Or maybe she'd open her eyes and realise she was just sinking into a muddy trench of water and was in her final moments.

But when she opened her eyes, Tara saw something quite surprising.

Surprising in its relative mundanity.

Which was a surprise in itself.

She was in a bedroom. The room looked… like it'd been made out of wood. She could smell the wood in the air, like the inside of a sauna. It looked fresh in here. Nice in here.

And it was warm, too.

She could hear something crackling. Looked up and saw a log burner in the corner of the room. Which really didn't seem wise in a building made out of wood.

But… this soft bedding.

This comforting warmth.

Where the hell was she?

Was this the waiting room to heaven after all?

She looked around the room. There were some day and night blinds over by the left of the bed, but they were closed. It was hard to tell whether it was night or day. It was… kind of light in here? So probably day.

She could smell something. A shitty smell on her skin. The muck from the field.

Fuck. What'd happened?

She looked over to the right when she saw something standing there.

Staring at her.

A dog.

A sheep dog.

Wagging its tail.

Tongue dangling out.

"Oh," Tara said. Her throat raspy. "Hey…"

The dog walked over to her. Let her pat its head a little.

"Let's… let's have a look at you then. Where did you come from?"

Naturally, the dog didn't say anything in return. Because it was a dog.

She patted its head. Its breath was a bit smelly, but to be honest, Tara was just kind of relieved to have someone here beside her. Someone here to make her feel less… alone.

"Who are you?" she whispered. "What is this place?"

She heard footsteps, then.

Footsteps.

Over by that door ahead of her.

Walking her way.

She tensed up.

Kept a hand on the dog's head.

Waited for whoever was about to walk through that door.

And in her mind's eye, she saw Jonno.

She saw him walking through that door.

Still alive.

Smirking.

And then she saw the door open, and someone else walked in.

Someone that wasn't Jonno.

Thank God.

It was a woman. An older woman. She looked about in her sixties but with really clear and healthy skin. She was smiling. An absolutely beaming smile stretched across her face.

"Hello, dear," she said. "Murphy isn't bothering you, is he?"

Tara opened her mouth to say something—anything—but found no words escaped.

"Come on, Murph," the woman said, whistling the dog over to her side. Which he did, and really obediently at that. "Sorry. He's very inquisitive, is all."

"It's—it's quite alright," Tara said. "Where..."

"Sorry," the woman said. "You'll have a lot of questions, won't you?"

"Just a few."

The woman walked over to the side of the bed. She had a glass of water and a glass of milk on a tray, as well as a couple of tablets and some cookies. Kind of reminded Tara of being a kid again. Milk and cookies before bed. "We pulled you out of the field. Really boggy in there. Absolute death trap. Lucky we spotted you when we did."

Shit. So she'd saved her. This woman had actually saved her.

"Where am I?"

"You're at the farm you were running towards when my husband, Gregg, spotted you. Well. One of the barns, anyway. Nicely renovated."

"It's lovely," Tara said.

"Thank you," the woman said, smiling. "Oh. Excuse my manners. Joyce."

"Tara," she said.

"Tara. You should get some food down you. And some water. And if you want a paracetamol or two, they'll probably not be a bad idea. As well as an antibiotic. Dread to think what you might've picked up out there."

Tara twisted round. Tried to sit up. But she was exhausted. So, so exhausted. "Where..."

"Where what, love?"

"There was... there was a kid," Tara said, the urgency of the situation coming back to her. "We were—we were trying to find Marky. And we saw a kid on your field, and... and..."

The woman frowned. "A kid?"

"A little boy."

"I'm sorry. But we... I can't think who that might be."

Shit. What if it was Marky? What if he'd sunk into the waterlogged ground, too?

"And you keep saying 'we', dear," Joyce said. "What do you mean by that?"

Tara frowned. "What?"

"When we pulled you out of the mud. You were... you were on your own..."

Everything drifted into the background.

"Rebecca," Tara said.

She tried to stand again.

But she was so tired.

So, so exhausted.

And her legs... her legs felt so weak.

"Calm down, dear."

"You need to—to find her."

"You're not making any sense."

"There was—there was someone else!" Tara shouted.

Joyce's eyes widened. Her face went pale. "Someone... else?"

"In the mud. Next to me. There was someone else. Rebecca. Please tell me you saved her. Please."

But Tara could see the answer on Joyce's face already.

"You have to go out there," Tara said. "You—you have to find her."

Joyce lowered her head. She stroked her dog.

"There's no time to—"

"I'm sorry, love," Joyce said. "But it's been... it's been a day. Whoever you were with... if they sunk in the mud, then they're... they're already gone."

CHAPTER TWENTY-FOUR

Sam saw the man standing in that window of the house and felt a shiver creep up his spine.

Because whoever this man was, it definitely wasn't Tristan.

It definitely wasn't *anyone* he knew.

"The others," Lydia said. Staring up towards that window. Eyes wide.

And on her face, a look of fear.

A look of renewed fear.

"It's—it's him," she said. "Tom. I—I told him to find his own place. I told him to—to find his own place, but he keeps on coming back. With his friends. With... with the bad people. With the others."

When she said those words, it all clicked into place for Sam.

The hairs on the back of his neck stood right on end.

'Cause he didn't know who this guy was.

And in normal times, he might not have jumped to conclusions so rapidly.

But the fact that Marky was missing.

The fact that Harvey was missing.

The fact that this poor old woman was out there in the woods, struggling on her own and fearing for the "others" in her home.

It all added up to something that needed investigating.

Urgently.

"You sit right here," Sam said, leading Lydia over towards her rotten wooden garden table. He pulled his jacket off, and he draped it over her shoulders.

"What're you doing?" she asked.

He looked back up at the attic window.

The man—Tom, as Lydia called him—was gone.

Sam's fists tightened. "I'm going to go find out what's happening here."

He took a deep breath, and he started to run when Lydia called for him.

"Be careful," she said. "He's dangerous. His—his friends are dangerous. They hurt people. They hurt me. Please be careful!"

And her desperation made him wince.

Her fear made him wince.

He had no idea what the situation was here. And he had no idea what this poor woman had been through at the hands of Tom and his "friends."

He didn't even know how much of what she was saying was actually true.

Because she *was* struggling mentally. That much was clear to see.

But this man. In the attic.

Staring out onto the garden.

Where had he come from?

Why had he been keeping such a low profile?

He ran across the boggy garden. Onto the patio.

And then he went to yank open the kitchen door when he noticed something that made his stomach sink.

The kitchen door.

It was closed.

It was locked.

He tried the handle again. Banged on the glass. "Tristan?"

Nothing.

Fuck.

He banged on the glass again, trying to get the attention of those inside. "Tristan! Leonard! Millie! Anyone!"

But the more he knocked, the more he realised nobody was answering.

He went to knock again when he saw him appear at the lounge door.

"Leonard," Sam said. "Hey, buddy. Let me in."

But Leonard just stood there.

Leonard just stared.

Peeking around the doorway.

"Leonard," Sam said. "You—you need to let me in, buddy."

"Daddy said don't leave the room."

"Where is your dad?"

"He's upstairs," Leonard said. "He said not to leave the room."

Fuck. So Tristan was upstairs while the kids were downstairs.

And upstairs also was this guy. This Tom.

And the Others.

The ones who must've locked the kitchen door.

"Leonard, I need you to listen to me," Sam said. "I need you to come over here and unlock this door and let me in, okay? It's... it's really important."

Leonard stood there. Stared. Clearly just as stubborn as his bloody mother, then.

And then Sam had another idea.

"Is Millie there with you?"

Leonard nodded.

"Tell her. Tell her I'm here. Okay? Bring her to the door with you, and let me speak with her."

Leonard looked over his shoulder. Sam heard voices. Like Leonard was speaking to Millie.

And then Leonard looked back at him again. "I can't."

Sam frowned. "You—you can't?"

Leonard shook his head.

"Why can't you?"

"Because... because Gilly says I can't."

Gilly.

Sam felt cold.

Cold to the core.

Gilly.

Who the fuck was Gilly?

"Leonard," Sam said. "I need you to..."

And that's when Sam felt it.

Right behind him.

The unmistakable sharp end of a cold blade right against the back of his neck.

"Hello there," a voice whispered in his ear. "What seems to be the problem here?"

CHAPTER TWENTY-FIVE

Tara lay there on the bed and tried to wrap her head around what she'd just been told about Rebecca.

It was comfortable in this room. Warm. Too fucking warm, in a way. The bedding she was lying against was so soft, and it kept on making her want to drift off to sleep. It was a real struggle staying awake.

But she felt pathetic dozing off. Her people needed her. Fuck. Tristan would be back at the house, wondering where the hell she was and where the hell Rebecca was.

And then there was Sam, too.

'Cause even though he and Rebecca weren't married anymore, she was his wife once. And they seemed on relatively decent terms considering they were exes.

She thought of Jonno.

Blowing his brains out right in front of her.

If only he'd taken the breakup quite as gracefully.

The dog, Murph, sat at Tara's side. She stroked his head. It just gave her some sort of comfort. Made her feel less... well, alone right now. She looked around this beautiful converted barn, and while she felt comfortable and warm here, she felt a bit pathetic, too.

Because the last thing she knew, Marky had gone missing.

For all she knew, he was still missing.

In danger.

And Rebecca was... Rebecca was gone.

And where was she?

She was lying in bed in a comfy barn conversion.

She swallowed a sickly lump in her throat. She felt dozy, caught in a thick brain fog that wouldn't shift. Maybe she'd caught an infection from that water and all that muck.

Shit. She thought back to the moment she lost the battle. The moment her mouth opened and she let that horrible water and muck slip between her lips.

It seemed like a dream. A distant nightmare that hadn't actually happened to her. Just something she remembered right in the back of her mind. Something she wanted to forget.

Shit. There were lots of things she wanted to forget these last few days.

Things she would never, ever be able to forget.

But she wasn't going to lie here and feel sorry for herself.

She was going to get up.

She was going to get out of this barn.

She was going to thank Joyce and her husband—whoever he was, 'cause Tara still hadn't met him yet—for getting her back on her feet.

And then she was going to find her friends again.

She went to climb out of bed with her heavy legs, sickness and nausea clawing at her stomach when she noticed the pills by the side of the bed.

She'd taken a couple of those antibiotics earlier with water when Joyce came in here.

But sitting here now, a little more awake, something struck her.

Those pills.

Little white pills.

The ones beside the antibiotics.

She thought they were paracetamol at first. Why wouldn't she?

But as she looked closer and saw the Ab logo on the side, she felt her body shiver.

They were sleeping pills.

She'd taken lots of them. Two at a time, every couple of hours.

And these pills were strong. Half a pill used to knock her out for the night when she struggled with depression in her teen years.

Two of these pills every couple of hours was enough to...

Make her feel nauseous.

Make her feel knackered.

And make her feel weak.

She heard shuffling over by the door.

The door opened.

Joyce stepped inside, smile on her face.

"Tara, dear," she said. "I've made you some lovely soup. Where do you think you're going? Definitely don't want to push yourself too much. Not just yet."

Tara watched Joyce walk across the room with that big, wide smile.

Another side effect of sleeping pill overdose was paranoia.

Was she just being paranoid?

Or what if...

She didn't know.

She didn't have a fucking clue.

"Tara?" Joyce said. Frowning a little. "Are you okay?"

Tara looked up at her. That chicken soup smelled so wholesome and warm, and delicious.

"The—the pills," Tara said.

"What about them?"

"You've been giving me sleeping pills?"

Joyce didn't even hesitate.

She nodded. "I told you. Paracetamol. Antibiotic. And one of Frank's sleeping pills every day. It'll help you relax."

"But—but I've had more than one."

"You haven't had more than one," Joyce said, laughing a little. "Look. You're here on my farm, and I'm looking after you. You just need to lie down and relax. Get yourself well rested. You've been through a lot. Trauma, and now you're not well at all."

She climbed back onto the bed. Fuck. Maybe she was just being paranoid. After all, Joyce hadn't shown any signs of being sinister, had she?

Joyce stroked Tara's hair out of her face in a strangely motherly way. "Relax. Get some more rest."

"My... my friends—"

"Can wait a few hours longer," Joyce said. "And then we can go find them together. You don't have to worry, okay? You're safe here. Lucky to be alive. You've been through a lot. Let yourself rest."

She patted Tara's shoulder.

Then she turned around, leaving the soup right there on the tray beside the bed.

Tara lay there.

Looked at the door Joyce was heading towards.

Maybe she could stomach a little soup.

Maybe a bit of food would help her relax just a little bit.

She went to grab the steaming hot bowl when suddenly she saw something.

Over at the door.

Just before Joyce stepped out, it caught her eye.

On a tray outside her room, Tara saw another bowl of soup.

Another glass of water.

And another little pile of pills.

Joyce turned around.

Smiled at Tara.

"Don't worry," she said. "You just relax."

And then she closed the door shut.

But as Tara lay there, feeling weaker and weaker as she held on to the soup, she couldn't get a horrible suspicion out of her mind.

Something was wrong here.

Something was very wrong.

Because who was that extra bowl of soup for?

Who was that extra glass of water for?

And who were those extra pills for?

CHAPTER TWENTY-SIX

J oyce walked out of the bedroom dear Tara was staying in and breathed a sigh of relief.

She knew that was close.

Far, far too close.

She couldn't afford to be so stupid and so complacent again.

She walked down the corridor, pushing her tray along. The soup smelled delicious. Chicken soup. She'd cooked it over a portable stove of Frank's. Bless him. He always used to buy all kinds of tools that he never used. He used to tease Joyce that she'd thank him for those purchases one day. And as reluctant as she was to accept it... she was beginning to realise Frank was right.

She walked further down the corridor and tried to wrap her head around the exchange she'd just had with Tara. Tara was intuitive. Most people wouldn't even ask a question about what medication they were on when they'd just been through a trauma like the one she had. She was smart. Clever. Just like her Elouise.

She knew she was right to have a good feeling about her.

She knew she was a gift from God.

And she knew, now more than ever, that she was going to be keeping her here.

Right here.

She thought back to the moment she'd pulled her out of that water.

Dragging her along back towards the farm.

Hearing that other sound behind her.

That other voice.

Begging.

She thought back to that moment, and she sighed.

She'd done what she could for Tara. She'd given her the medication she needed to take her pain away. She'd given her the antibiotics she needed to ease any infection.

And the sleeping pills...

She wanted to make her comfortable.

She wanted her to rest.

But she also didn't want her to go walking around.

She didn't want her getting out of bed and searching this place.

Because there were things Joyce didn't want Tara to see.

And it was very, very important she kept those things secret.

But more than anything, it was for Tara's own good.

She needed rest right now.

She needed sleep right now.

And if it took a few extra sleeping pills to help her, then that wasn't a problem.

She'd thank her later.

One day, in the future, she'd thank her.

She closed her burning eyes. It had been a tough few days managing the farm all by herself. And she knew there were things she would have to explain to Tara when she came around. Things she would have to be more honest and truthful about.

Things like the fact she might've seen a child after all.

Things like the fact that Frank was dead.

And that he had been dead for ten years.

And things like…

Well.

She hoped she wouldn't have to explain *that*.

She walked further down the corridor, and she caught a look at herself in the mirror.

She was old. So, so old.

How had she got this old so quickly?

It didn't seem a moment ago that she was walking across the fields, hand in hand with Elouise.

It didn't seem a moment ago that she sat by her bedside, staring at her, with her bald head, pale face, and gaunt features, squeezing her hand and praying for her to hold on, just to hold on.

It didn't seem a moment ago that Joyce pushed Frank down the stairs.

Heard his neck snap as he tumbled down those steps.

Heard his head crack like an egg as it slammed against the hard floor below.

It didn't seem a moment ago that she lost everything—but gained everything, too.

Her independence.

Her pride.

She walked away from the mirror.

Stood outside the next door on the corridor in this old barn conversion.

She took a deep breath and forced her widest smile.

And then she opened the door.

"Hello, Rebecca," she said. "How are you feeling, dear?"

CHAPTER TWENTY-SEVEN

Sam felt the blade to his neck, and he knew right away that he was fucked.

He saw Leonard standing there inside the house, through the window in the kitchen door. His wide eyes staring out at Sam. Or at the person behind him, holding the knife to his neck. Gilly. He'd said someone inside was called Gilly.

Which meant there was someone in there with them.

Someone was in the house.

The kids were in danger.

He felt that cold, sharp blade against the back of his neck.

"Don't move a fucking muscle," the bloke said. "Not if you don't want me to ram this blade right into your fucking throat."

Sam gritted his teeth. Fucking typical. These psychos must be the "others" Lydia spoke about. The ones this guy, Tom, was friends with. Whoever the hell Tom was and whatever the hell these people were doing.

Either way, it seemed like Lydia was right.

She wasn't completely crazy.

There were people here who were harming her.

And they were here now, too.

"What the fuck is your problem?" Sam said. Seeing the bloke's reflection in the glass.

"Our problem is that you're on our property."

"*Your* property? Or Lydia's here?"

"Don't get fucking smart with me, mate," the man said, pushing Sam against the door and pressing that knife to his neck even harder. "I'll end you. I'll end you if you get fucking cocky. Best thing you can do is shut the fuck up until I get Tom down here to figure out what we're gonna do with you."

Sam's stomach sank. So these people, whoever they were, had taken over Lydia's property. And now they were rounding up Sam's people. They were rounding them up, and they were going to kick them out—or worse.

And all the while... Harvey and Wayne were in the woods behind the house somewhere.

As for Marky?

These people must have something to do with his disappearance.

But what?

What did they want?

What were they trying to achieve?

"Get on your knees."

Sam sighed. "I'm not getting on my knees."

A kick to the back of his leg—his weak leg—hard, making him stagger. "I'm not fucking asking politely. Get on your fucking knees right this fucking second, or I'll jab you in the fucking neck."

Sam shook his head. "Welcoming. Good to see people are really banding together in the end times, you know."

He started to crouch down when he saw the figure appear behind Leonard inside.

A woman.

Holding Millie's hand.

The woman looked scruffy and messy. She was missing a few teeth and was desperately thin.

Millie looked afraid.

"On your knees," the bloke said. Absolutely reeked of weed he did. "I won't ask you again."

Sam shifted his focus on the window to the man behind him, to his reflection.

He was skinny too.

Clearly didn't have a lot of muscle to him.

And maybe that could work in Sam's favour.

He crouched even further down and saw the rock by the side of the kitchen door.

"You know something?" Sam said.

"What the fuck you saying now?"

Sam held his breath. "You should be careful who you mess with."

He grabbed the rock and swung it at the man's head.

Hard.

The rock cracked against the man's face.

Sent him flying back in a bloody heap.

Blood pooling down from his nose and his eyes.

"Fuck!"

And then, before he could even think, Sam turned around and threw that rock through the kitchen window.

The glass smashed everywhere.

He reached in.

Turned the key, nipping his arm on sharp loose glass in the process.

And then he opened the kitchen door, and he ran towards the lounge.

And then he saw this Gilly woman in front of him.

She was holding Leonard and Millie around the throat.

Hard.

"Let them fucking go," Sam said.

"You don't give the orders here."

"They're kids. And you're going to let them fucking go. Or trust me. You'll rue the fucking day."

Gilly stood there.

Narrowed her eyes.

Holding on to their throats.

Not budging.

"Okay," Sam said, grabbing a kitchen knife from the side. "We'll do it the hard way, then."

He stormed through the kitchen towards that woman when suddenly he felt something smash over his head from the right.

He tumbled to the floor.

His right ear ringing like mad, and blood pouring from his right eye socket.

Someone else in the kitchen.

"Fuck."

He looked up.

Looked up at that other junkie-looking prick standing there.

At Gilly, who held on to the kids.

And then at the bloody face of the bloke he'd attacked in the garden.

"Let's put the fucker down," the bloke from the garden said, spitting a bloody blob onto Sam.

He lifted his knife with his shaking hand and swung it towards Sam when he heard footsteps in the hallway.

"Nobody's putting *anyone* down," a voice said.

The man looked up.

The other two looked around.

Footsteps.

Walking towards the kitchen.

Sam looked up, and he saw someone right there.

Standing at the doorway.

The man from the attic window.

"Hello there," he said. Staring right into Sam's eyes. "I'm Tom. I think we've got a bit of a problem here, don't you?"

And he wasn't alone

He was with Tristan.

And he had a knife to Tristan's throat.

CHAPTER TWENTY-EIGHT

Tara sat on the edge of the bed and knew that no matter how weak or exhausted she felt right now, she needed to get out of here.

And she needed to get out of here fast.

She had no idea what time of day it was. No idea what the weather was like. Only the fact she couldn't hear the rain hammering against the roof of this converted barn probably meant it wasn't as torrential as it had been the last few days.

The door stared back at her, right ahead of her. She had no idea whether it was open or whether it was locked. Why would it be locked? She wasn't this woman's prisoner.

But then...

Maybe that wasn't entirely true.

The woman had been giving her sleeping pills—more than she claimed. Tara was sure of it. She wasn't just being paranoid—she was certain.

And if she was giving her an overdose of sleeping pills, what else was she doing that Tara didn't know about?

It was silent in here. Silent but for the sound of the wood

crackling away in that fire. And for Murph, the dog, bless him, snoring away. If Tara got away from this place, she was going to make damned sure she took him with her. She didn't want him being stuck here with a psycho.

If that's what was happening here.

It was all still just suspicion.

It was all still just speculation.

But she had a bad feeling. A really bad feeling her hunch was right.

The room smelled of logs burning. A comforting smell. But a smell that made a shudder creep up her spine and a shiver creep down her arms. She could taste a weird medicinal tang in her throat. And vomit, too—the slight hint of vomit on her lips.

And her body was so weak.

It was so exhausted.

She didn't feel like she could put one foot in front of another.

But she had to.

She simply had to.

She'd seen the tray outside the room.

The tray with the soup.

The tray with more tablets.

Just like the tray Joyce brought in here for her.

Why would she have another tray like that?

What wasn't she telling her?

Was there... someone else?

Was Rebecca alive after all?

She didn't know. And she wasn't going to find out the answers if she didn't get out of here—fast.

She climbed out of bed, but moving was hard. Her muscles were so weak, and she was so shaky. She felt like she had done when she'd had the flu a few years ago. Always dismissed people when they said they had the flu. Thought it was just an overblown cold.

But that flu left her feeling like she was dying.

Like if someone offered her a pill and told her they would take all the pain away, she would've snapped their hands off in an instant.

She tried to breathe deeply.

Tried to put one foot in front of the other.

Her head ached.

Her muscles got weaker and weaker.

She grew dizzier by the second.

Just a few more steps. Just... just a few more steps...

She walked further and further towards the door when she heard something outside.

Footsteps.

She stood there.

Frozen to the spot.

What if Joyce came in here?

What if she found her snooping around?

She stood there, waiting for the footsteps to get closer.

Tried to think of an excuse, of an answer, of a reason; her brain totally foggy, everything totally blurry...

And then the footsteps passed by her room.

Right on by.

She let go of her breath, the tension in her body at breaking point.

She walked further along the wooden floor.

Closer to that door.

She was so close.

So, so close.

She walked up to the door.

Stopped.

Waited a few seconds.

Strained to see if she could hear anything outside.

She couldn't hear a thing.

She reached for the handle.

Her hand shaking.

Grabbed the handle.

Strained to hear again.

And then, when she was sure there was nobody out there, she tried to lower the handle.

But the handle didn't budge.

Her stomach sank.

Horror kicked in.

The slim hope she had that this wasn't something sinister dissipated in an instant.

And a realisation dawned on her.

She was a prisoner.

She was Joyce's prisoner.

She tried the handle again a few more times.

But still, it was locked.

Still, it was completely locked.

She looked around the room.

Looked for another way out.

The window.

She had to try the window.

She rushed over to it as fast as her weak, ailing body would allow.

Tried to lift the blind.

But the blind was stuck.

It wasn't just jammed or anything.

It was actually *pinned* to the window frame.

She stood there as the horror of the situation dawned on her more and more by the second.

As fear completely engulfed her.

She was weak.

And she was a prisoner.

And she was trapped in here.

She looked around the room for something she could use.

Anything she could use.

But there was nothing.

Nothing she could use as a lock pick.

Nothing she could use to try and open the window.

Nothing.

She looked around, and she saw the fire.

An idea came to mind.

A horrible idea.

An idea that might backfire.

But an idea she had to try.

She walked over to the wooden log burner.

Looked down at the logs.

At those flames.

And as she stood there in this room made out of wood... a morbid idea developed right before her eyes.

An idea that might be risky.

An idea that might be so, so dangerous.

But an idea she was going to have to try.

She reached towards the door of the log burner.

Heard Murph whining behind her.

"It's—it's okay," she said. "She won't... she won't let you burn in here. She won't let either of us burn in here."

She reached in towards the heat of the logs.

Reached in to try and grab one.

To set this place ablaze.

"She won't let us burn," Tara muttered as her hand got closer to the burning log. "She won't let us—"

"Who won't?"

A voice.

A voice that made Tara freeze.

She turned around.

And she saw her.

Joyce was standing at the door.

Her arms were folded.

And she was holding a syringe in one hand.

She wasn't smiling.

Not this time.

"What do you think you're doing?" she asked.

CHAPTER TWENTY-NINE

S am looked up at Tom, who held the blade to Tristan's throat, and he knew this shit wasn't going to be easy.

Of course it wasn't going to be fucking easy.

Nothing was *ever* fucking easy these days.

The kitchen was dark. It was gloomy outside, raining again. The kitchen was quiet. Quiet, but for the muffled cries of the kids. Of Leonard and of Millie, who were clearly scared.

And of Tristan.

Hand to his mouth.

Struggling.

He lay there on his stomach. Tom and four others surrounded him, including the prick he'd bashed over the head from outside. He thought about Lydia. Poor woman was right about these people—these "others", as she called them. They were savage pricks. He didn't know who they were or what their endgame was, but he'd seen enough to know he didn't want anything else to do with them.

And then he thought about Rebecca and Tara. They'd been a while. Where were they? He hoped they were okay. Fuck, he could really do with them right now.

And then there was Wayne.

Harvey.

Marky.

He hadn't seen them for a while, either.

Part of him wanted them to stay away so they didn't get caught up and embroiled in whatever was going down here.

And another part of him really needed some help right now.

He lay there, flat on the floor. No knife in hand anymore. Nothing to defend himself with. Nothing to fight with.

"So," Tom said. "Seems we're in a bit of a pickle here, doesn't it?"

Sam stared up at Tom. "The only pickle I see is the fact you've got my friend there with a knife to his throat. And that *your* friend is threatening two kids."

"Don't take the moral high ground," Tom said. "You're here, in my home, uninvited."

"*Your* home?"

"Don't let that crazy old bitch get to your head," Tom said. "This place is mine. My father was going to leave it to me. He was going to leave *everything* to me. But then he leaves it to her instead—that gold-digger who could never, ever replace my mum. And... well. Since I found myself in a bit of trouble, I figured this house was big enough to support a few of my friends, too."

"So that's what's going on here," Sam said. "You're a bunch of squatters. And now *you're* getting uppity about the fact we're staying in your home."

"Call me what you want," Tom said. "I'm the one with the blade to your friend's throat."

Sam looked up at him. He didn't know what to say or what to do. He just knew he needed to be careful. "What do you want?"

"What do I want?" Tom asked. "You could start by apologising."

"Apologising?"

"Coming in here uninvited. Treating this place like it's your own."

"That's it? An apology? That's all you're after?"

"It'd be a start."

Sam sighed. "Look. I'm sorry for fucking sleeping in your home without asking your permission. Better now?"

"You've got attitude on you, haven't you?"

"Why do I get the feeling you're not being completely straight with me about what you want?"

Tom smiled. "Because you're a man who clearly knows how the world works."

He loosened his grip on Tristan. Lowered the knife just a little.

"You look like a competent bloke."

"I'll take that as a compliment."

Tom smirked. "The rest of your people... they look strong, too."

"Where are you going with this?"

"I'd say you owe me and my friends here."

"Owe you?"

"There's a whole world of supplies out there. And, truth be told, we ain't so keen on going exploring. People like us, we're not strong enough. Not yet, anyway. We need help. So if you'd be kind enough to help us... well, that'd make a world of difference."

Sam shook his head. "That's really it? We're going to help you?"

"Exactly that."

"And if I say 'fuck off'?"

"Then maybe I'll not bother telling you where the missing little boy is."

Sam's skin turned cold.

Millie's eyes widened. "Marky?"

Tom smiled.

"I'll tell you what I want you to do for us. And I'll keep it very simple and very specific. There's a farm just up the road. Proper weird woman runs the place. She has tons of supplies. Things that'd go a hell of a long way. More specifically… medication."

"Drugs," Sam said.

"Call them what you want," Tom said. "As long as you get 'um for me and my friends, it doesn't really matter."

Sam gritted his teeth. Marky. These fuckers knew about Marky. And they were using him as a bargaining chip. They were smarter than they were letting on—and that infuriated him.

"She used to look after her daughter," Tom said. "Dying of cancer. She tried everything. Stole all sorts of meds. Anything you can think of, she's got it. Including methadone. Morphine."

"I think I know where you're going with this."

He lifted the knife to Tristan's neck. "We don't know exactly where she keeps 'em, which is where you come in. You have a little chat with her. You get us our supplies. Enough to last us. And I'll let you all go. And I'll tell you what I know. About the boy."

Sam lay there shaking. He was furious. Raging.

But at the same time, he wanted to keep his emotions in check.

Wanted to keep them under control.

Wanted to play this right.

Just right.

He lay there on the kitchen floor.

Looked at Millie, the tears rolling down her face.

At Tristan, knife to his throat.

At Leonard, his mother's eyes staring back at him.

And then at Tom.

He looked into his eyes.

"Okay," Sam said.

Tom frowned. Like he wasn't expecting that. "What?"

"I said 'okay'," Sam said. "We'll get what you want from the farm. And you'll let us go and tell us everything you know about Marky."

Tom's smile widened.

He lowered his knife.

"Good," he said.

He walked over to Sam.

Held out a hand.

Sam didn't take it. He pushed himself to his feet himself.

"And if you even think about trying anything..." Tom said. "The kid's done for."

CHAPTER THIRTY

"What do you think you're doing, dear?"

Tara stood in the converted barn right by the fire. She could feel the intense heat of those flames so close to her.

And she could see Joyce.

Right there.

Right there by the door.

Staring at her.

Syringe in hand.

And Tara didn't know what to say. She felt weak. Her legs were like jelly. Her head was spinning. Every time she *tried* to think... she just felt completely caught up in a thick, impenetrable fog.

She just stood there and stared at Joyce as Joyce stared back at her.

"I... I was..." Tara started.

But she could see where Joyce was looking.

She could see how her gaze shifted from Tara's face to the wood burner beside her.

She could see Tara reaching for one of those logs.

She looked back up at Tara.

Right into her eyes.

"Dear?"

"I was... I was just turning the logs."

"With your bare hands?"

Tara gritted her teeth. Fuck. What even *was* she trying to do? Burn the place down just to get this woman's attention?

And besides.

Why was she acting so compliant when she knew damn well this woman wasn't being straight with her?

When she knew damn well this woman was keeping her prisoner?

"You look... unwell," Joyce said. "I think we really underestimated how sick you are. You need to rest."

And then she started walking towards Tara.

That syringe in her hand.

Tara stepped back.

"You don't come another step near me with any medication."

Joyce frowned. "Dear?"

"Stop that. Just... just stop that. What the fuck is going on here?"

"I don't quite understand."

"The door. The locked door. And—and the other tray. The other tray with the soup. What the fuck is happening here?"

Joyce looked shocked at Tara's words and winced every time she cursed. "The door... the door is not locked, love. Why on earth would I lock the door?"

"Don't bullshit me—"

"Please," Joyce said. "You're—You've been through a lot. You're acting... erratic. Just... just get back on the bed, please. For your own safety."

Tara stood there by the fire. "I'm going nowhere."

Joyce took another step towards her. "If you don't... I'm going to have to defend myself."

"Defend yourself?"

"You're being erratic. You're being threatening. And the way you're standing by that fire... it worries me. Please. This... I'm trying to help you."

Tara stood there, and for a split second, she wondered.

What if Joyce was telling the truth?

What if it was her who was being erratic?

She looked at this whole situation through Joyce's perspective, through her eyes, and for a moment, for just a moment, she saw exactly what Joyce saw.

"I appreciate your help," Tara said. Softening her stance somewhat. "And I appreciate all you've done for me. But—but I've decided I'm done here. I've got friends out there. Friends who need help. Friends who'll be worried about me. So if... if you're really telling me I've nothing to worry about here and that all this is in my head... you'll let me go. Right now."

She saw Joyce's mouth moving. Saw her struggling to find the words.

And Tara fully expected her to stand in her way.

She fully expected her to resist.

But something surprising happened.

Joyce nodded.

She stepped aside.

"I—I really think you should get some more rest and get yourself well. I am worried about you. After what you've been through. But... but you are not my prisoner. You can leave whenever you want, love. I just... I just worry about you. That's all."

Tara had to admit she was surprised. She didn't expect that at all. She expected her to stand in her way. Expected her to obstruct her.

And to be honest, it made her worry a little bit.

What if she really was telling the truth?

What if Joyce really did have her best interests at heart all along?

She gulped. And then she nodded. Walking towards the door,

past Joyce. She saw Murphy looking up at her. Tilting his head. Wagging his tail.

"I'll be sorry to see you go," Joyce said. "Really."

Tara nodded at her. She felt a bit of a dick, to be honest. "I'm grateful for what you did for me. I appreciate it. Really."

Joyce looked at the floor. Nodded.

Tara kept on walking through the door. The open door. The corridor, right ahead of her, waiting for her to walk through it.

"Which way?" Tara asked.

"First right."

Tara stepped out of the door. Looked back again.

Saw Joyce standing there in the room.

Murphy by her side.

That comfortable, warm room that she had to admit she kind of missed already.

The soft, inviting bed, so comfortable, calling her back.

"Stay well," Tara said.

"Yes," Joyce said. "You too."

She turned around.

Walked down the corridor.

Walked towards that door on the right.

The door just like hers.

She just wanted to get out of here now.

She just wanted to get away.

She could feel herself getting stronger with every step.

She had to take advantage of this moment.

She reached the door.

Stopped in front of it.

Looked down the corridor.

Nobody in sight.

She felt her jaw tense.

Was she making a mistake?

Should she be staying here?

She shook her head.

Tried to shake through that brain fog.

"Come on," she muttered. "Time to go home."

She lowered the handle and pushed the door open.

She expected a gust of wind, or a burst of light from the sun, or something like that.

But... she didn't experience that at all.

She saw something different entirely.

There was someone lying there on a bed.

A bed, just like the one she'd been on.

A room, just like the one she'd been in.

And on that bed...

"Re—Rebecca?" Tara said.

Rebecca's eyes widened. "Tara? I thought you were..."

And then, the next thing Tara knew, she felt a sharp scratch on her neck and a burst of warmth sinking into her skin.

Joyce was here.

She had the syringe needle buried into her neck.

And she looked mad.

Really fucking mad.

"I don't think so, dear," Joyce said. "Not so fast."

And as much as Tara tried to push back, as much as she tried to fight... her limbs failed her, and she sunk down to the floor below.

CHAPTER THIRTY-ONE

S am stepped out of Lydia's house, Tristan and the kids in front of him, and he knew he didn't have a choice in what he was doing.

Not if they wanted any chance of getting Marky back.

The skies were grey. The rain was falling a little. Hopefully, it wasn't going to get as bad as last week. He smelled the cold, fresh air. Tasted an acidic tang on his lips. Always got it when he was nervous. Anxious. Like a precursor to vomit. He'd tasted it a lot when he'd had his relationship breakdown with Rebecca. A big part of the reason why he gulped so many beers down to mask the taste.

He could see the fields in the distance. And he could see that farm, too. The farm way off in the distance.

The farm Tom and his squatting friends wanted him to go to.

The farm he wanted him to steal drugs from.

The farm he wanted him to raid, and if he did, he'd give him the information they needed about Marky's whereabouts.

He could hear movement behind him. Coughing. Looked around and saw Tom at the door. Smirking. His friends behind him in this derelict old house, watching him closely.

And Sam felt so fucking sorry for Lydia. This house had fallen to ruin. This sponger of a stepson had taken her for a ride. What-ever differences the pair of them had, all Sam saw was a bitter stepson who felt jealous that this woman had stolen something he thought he had a right to. A bloke who hadn't done a day's work in his life, who had sponged off the good fortune of the others around him. Literally Sam's least favourite sort of person.

And now he'd made Sam his bitch.

Or so he thought.

He looked into Tom's eyes, and he saw Tristan shaking his head.

"What?" Sam asked.

"Is this the right call?" Tristan said.

Sam shrugged. "Do you see another way?"

"What if they don't..."

"What if they don't what?"

"What if they're bullshitting? And they don't even know anything about Marky?"

Sam looked back at them. "It doesn't change anything about what we're going to do."

"What do you mean by that?"

Sam put a hand on Millie's shoulder.

He stood there with the man his ex-wife loved—who the love of his life loved—and weirdly, unexpectedly, he felt like they were standing together.

"We're going to get the drugs we need from this farm," Sam said. "We're going to bring them back here. We're going to give them what they want. And we're going to find out what happened to Marky. And where he is."

And then he looked at Tristan.

"And even if we don't... it doesn't change what happens next."

Tristan stared at him. Wide-eyed. "What happens next?"

Sam smiled. Glanced back over at Tom and his bunch of junkie cunts.

"We're going to make those lowlife bastards regret ever crossing us," Sam said.

CHAPTER THIRTY-TWO

Tara opened her eyes.

She was in the bed again. The warm, comfy bed. Only... No. This wasn't the same bedroom. It was slightly different somehow. It felt more cramped. It felt like she wasn't alone.

She couldn't see. Her vision was all blurry and faded and grey. She felt tired. So, so tired. But she knew she couldn't fall asleep. She knew she couldn't drift off because she was worried what might happen to her if she did.

She could hear something. Something muffled and faded approaching her across the room.

She could smell the burning logs.

Taste them in the air.

Logs, and something else.

Something like blood.

She blinked a few times to try and get her vision back when she saw someone beside her.

Someone was lying there, right beside her.

And after a few blinks Tara realised who it was.

Exactly who it was.

"Re..." she started.

But she couldn't finish.

She was too exhausted to even speak.

To even say her name.

Rebecca was lying on the bed right beside her. She looked... peaceful. Resting. Like she was comfortable. Like she was warm and safe and okay.

Only...

When Tara squinted, she saw that wasn't the case.

It wasn't the case at all.

Rebecca looked worried.

She looked panicked.

She looked afraid.

And she looked like she was just as debilitated as Tara was.

And Tara knew why.

The reason why was walking right towards them.

Tara turned over. It hurt to even move at this point. Hurt to twist her neck.

She looked up and saw someone walking towards her.

A blur at this point. A distant blur, right ahead, getting closer.

She squinted. Not that she had to, really. She knew who this woman was. She knew exactly who she was.

She watched her get closer.

Watched that blurry cloud approaching her.

And she tried to shift back.

Tried to edge away from her.

But it was no use.

She was tired and exhausted, and she couldn't move another inch.

She saw Joyce getting closer to her.

And closer.

And with all the strength in her weak, failing body, she reached out and took Rebecca's hand.

Squeezed it as tightly as her limp fingers could.

Rebecca squeezed back.

Gently, but enough.

Whatever they were facing, they were facing it together.

Joyce stepped into clear view.

She was smiling. Her smile was a little more shaky. And to be honest, her entire demeanour seemed somewhat more... manic, for want of a better word.

But she was here, and she was smiling and stinking like TCP again.

"Hello, my dears," she said. "Did you both have a good rest?"

Tara tried to speak. She tried to shout. Fuck, she tried to lunge forward and throttle this cunt.

But there was nothing left in the tank.

Nothing at all.

"Good," Joyce said. "You needed it. You were getting... delusional. Oh well. As you'll see... I wasn't quite honest with the pair of you. But you have to know why it was. I just—I just wanted the best for you. I had your best interests at heart, not telling you the truth about each other. But I... I fear I've made a grave mistake. I fear you'll never trust me again. And that's why it has to be... this way."

She reached for Tara's leg.

Started stroking the inside of her shin.

Rubbing her fingers up and down the hairs on the inside of Tara's legs, which she hadn't had the time to shave since the power went out.

"My dear Elouise used to be a wandering soul, too. Went wandering far too often in the fields. I never used to like it. Spent far too long around those pylons. They give you cancer, you know? They gave my dear Elouise cancer. And—and it took her from me. The cancer took her from me. And then..."

She stopped. Shook her head. For a moment, her mask had slipped. But it was back now. Back, with a smile.

And those beaming eyes peering right at Tara.

"You're good girls," she said. "I know that. You're curious. And —and I understand you want to see your friends again. I really, really do. But... but we don't want you wandering. We don't want you going anywhere that might put you in danger. Mummy... Mummy doesn't want that for her princess at all."

She felt that hand move further up her leg.

Up to the inside of her thigh.

Squeeze, just a little.

And it made Tara want to vomit in her mouth.

And then Joyce let go with those rough hands and stood up.

She reached over to the tray by her side.

And on that tray, Tara saw something that made her freeze.

Another syringe.

Only this time...

This time, the syringe was filled with a darker fluid.

An almost green tone to it.

Joyce lifted it up. "This... this might not be pleasant. Not for... not for a little while. But it'll make sure you don't go walking again. Make sure you won't get yourself in any danger. I gave—I gave it to Elouise when I took her from the hospital. But—but I gave her too much. I won't make the same mistake with you. You'll be okay. I promise you'll be okay."

She pushed the needle to Tara's neck.

Looked right into her eyes.

Stroked her hair from her damp forehead.

"Just relax, my dear. Relax. It'll all be okay. Everything... everything will be okay."

And then she pushed the needle against Tara's neck and started to press the fluid into her.

CHAPTER THIRTY-THREE

Sam stood outside the farm and tensed his fists.

It was rainy again. Really rainy. The fields were an absolute boggy mess. It was so quiet. Quiet, but for the sound of the crows and the seagulls. He kept on thinking about Tara and Rebecca. Where the hell were they? They'd just gone up the road to investigate. To see if they could find any trace of Marky.

But they were gone. They were nowhere to be seen.

And the more time passed, the more concerned Sam grew.

'Cause what if they went back to the house?

They could look after themselves. Sam knew that much. He wasn't trying to patronise them or belittle them or anything. They were both tough—way fucking tougher than he was, he was starting to realise.

But even so.

Tom and his merry band of junkie cunts didn't look like the sort of people who would be very welcoming.

Or rather, they might be too welcoming.

Worryingly so.

He didn't want to think about that. Didn't want to entertain it as an option.

He just wanted to get inside this farm and investigate.

Truth be told, he felt a bit more uncertain about this place. Tom told him an old woman lived here. Crazy old woman. Tons of medication for her dead daughter or something.

But what if there was more to it?

What if this was some kind of setup?

What if there were things in here Sam and Tristan weren't prepared for?

And then there were the kids.

He looked down at Millie and Leonard.

Were they supposed to just go walking in there together?

What alternative did they have?

"You should wait out here with the kids," Sam said. "While I go in there and investigate."

Tristan looked right at Sam. "I'm not... entirely sure that's a great idea."

"And a better idea's going inside with them? It could be dangerous in there. We've no idea what we're walking into."

"It could be dangerous out here," Tristan said. "One thing's for sure. I'm not... I'm not leaving anyone anywhere anymore. We stick together. It's—it's how it has to be."

Sam opened his mouth to argue, to protest. He thought of Wayne. Out there in the woods behind the house, wherever he was, searching for Marky. He hoped to God Wayne was okay. And he hoped to God even more that Harvey was okay.

He tried to picture what Wayne would say if he knew they were out here with his daughter. If anything happened to her... fuck, he dreaded to think.

He felt like he was betraying Wayne by even being here.

But what other choice did he have?

He turned around to Tristan again. He knew it was a bold call either way. And one that could backfire.

But he was making this call.

He was going to own it, one way or another.

"I'm asking you to wait here," Sam said. "If you come inside… I'm worried what might happen."

"Leonard's my boy," Tristan said. "And I don't want him coming into any danger."

"But Millie's not your daughter. I made a promise. A promise to Wayne to look after her. To protect her. And I don't intend on failing him."

Tristan looked right into Sam's eyes. He looked torn. Like he didn't know what to do or what to say.

"You know it's right," Sam said. "You shouldn't come in here. You—you need to wait outside. And if anything's amiss at all— anything—then I won't be far away. Okay?"

Tristan opened his mouth. Closed it. And then he nodded. "She always said you were brave. To a fault."

"She said that?"

Tristan smiled. "Yeah. Said she kind of liked that I was the total opposite. I'm sure it wasn't meant offensively. Just… different types for different times, right?"

Sam thought about Rebecca speaking about him to her new husband. It seemed weird. They used to be so intertwined. Never used to argue about anything serious. Even at the end… they didn't use to argue. And maybe that was part of the problem, in a way. Maybe if he'd argued some more, what happened between them wouldn't've had to happen.

"Well, right now, staying right here with the kids is the main thing. The most important thing. You're doing a great job so far."

Tristan smiled at that. He looked genuinely grateful. He was a nice bloke. A wet bloody lettuce but a nice bloke.

"As are you," Tristan said.

Sam turned around to the farm.

Took a deep breath.

Thought of this poor, batty old woman he was about to steal

drugs from, all to fuel some junkie crew's addiction, and he wasn't sure how good a guy he was at all.

He went to take a step towards that farm when he heard something from the converted barns right at the side of the farm.

Sam heard a scream.

CHAPTER THIRTY-FOUR

Tara felt the needle pierce into her neck, and at that moment, a pure, unfiltered dose of fear crept into her bloodstream.

Fear, and whatever the fuck this Joyce psycho was trying to inject into her.

The room was all blurry and distant. She was absolutely terrified. She wanted to get up off this bed. She wanted to beat the shit out of Joyce and then get the fuck out of the room and out of the barn. She wanted so fucking much to escape this place and get back to her people—back to her friends.

But the sharp needle in her neck.

And Joyce's thumb, pushing that fluid into her...

"Don't worry," Joyce said. The stench of TCP seeping from her body and her breath. "It'll all be okay soon. You don't have to worry about a thing, my love. Not anymore..."

And Tara wanted to fight. She felt hopeless. Weak. Trapped not by the confines of her mind anymore but by the confines of her body itself.

She had to stand up for herself.

She had to fight.

But she couldn't.

She just couldn't.

She held on to Rebecca's hand. Rebecca was right by her side on the bed. She knew it must be fucking terrifying to witness. To watch. Because it was going to happen to her soon, too.

Rebecca was going to be next. And the scariest part was that there was nothing she could do about it. She was just as trapped as Tara was. She was just as restricted as Tara was.

She was just as completely and utterly fucked as Tara was.

She felt Rebecca's fingers against hers. Cold, shaky fingers.

And she realised how weird this was.

Holding the hand of the woman Sam loved so dearly.

The woman she was pretty sure she should feel a little bit envious of because of the connection she once had with Sam...

And yet she felt total love for her.

She felt total respect for her.

Total appreciation for her.

She held on to her hand as Joyce kept pressing that needle in, and she braced for the darkness...

And then she heard something snap.

The needle.

The needle in her neck.

Snapping.

And all the cold fluid from inside the syringe spilled over her neck and face.

A medicinal taste touching her lips.

"Oh gosh," Joyce said. "Clumsy me. Bear with me, dear. Let me get another one."

She saw Joyce turn away, humming to herself.

Heard her walking across the floor to the other side of the room.

She looked around on the tray beside her, right beside the bed, and she saw something that caught her eye.

A pair of scissors.

She looked at those scissors, and an idea grew in her mind.

The scissors.

Joyce.

Still humming.

Still right at the other side of the room.

Did she have time to grab them?

Did she have the strength to even do anything with them if she did?

There was only one way to find out.

She reached out.

Reached out for the scissors.

Reached out to grab them.

To grab them so she could attack Joyce and she could end this madness.

She could—

And then Joyce appeared.

Right above her.

Staring down at her.

Looking at her hand as it got closer to those scissors.

She moved the scissors just out of Tara's reach.

Looked down at Tara and smiled.

"I don't think you'll be needing those," she said. "Do you?"

She pumped a little liquid out of the new syringe.

Then she put her hand against Tara's neck and moved the needle towards her.

"Hold still, my love. It'll be over soon. All the pain will be over soon..."

Tara didn't think anymore.

She didn't second guess herself.

She didn't doubt herself.

She just acted on instinct now.

On pure instinct.

She swung around and bit Joyce on the hand.

Hard.

Joyce let out a wild scream.

The syringe tumbled from her fingers.

And Tara clamped down.

Clamped down on that hard skin and the flesh beneath for dear life.

Clamped down, sinking her teeth into the skin.

Sinking them in so much as Joyce smacked her across the neck.

Sinking them in until she tasted blood.

Joyce yanked her hand away. Staggered back. Clutched her hand. Bleeding out. "You witch," she said. "You—you aren't what I thought you were. You aren't my—my Elouise. You aren't my baby."

Tara sat upright with all the strength she could muster. Then she forced herself to her feet. Wobbly and uneven, but standing. "No," she said.

She reached down to the syringe on the floor.

Picked it up.

Walked over to Joyce.

"No, I'm not."

She pumped a little of the fluid out of the needle.

Grabbed Joyce by her thin, straw-like hair.

"I'm the person you shouldn't have fucked with."

And then she buried the needle into Joyce's neck.

Hard.

She pushed.

Pushed that fluid in.

Pushed it right into the vein as blood squirted out of her neck.

And then she pushed her back to the floor.

Almost immediately, Joyce started frothing at the mouth. Saliva, first. Then blood.

Her eyes were wide and bloodshot.

Her breathing was raspy.

She was bleeding from her ears.

And there was a patch of blood emerging around her arse, where she was bleeding out.

Tara stood over her and watched her writhe around the floor, dying.

She watched as she lifted her hand.

And when she did... she was back there again.

A child again.

By the pond again.

"Tara?"

A voice.

A voice right at the door.

There was someone here.

There was...

Tara looked up, and she saw him standing right there.

Staring in the room at the scene in front of him.

"Sam," Tara said.

He stood there. Looked at Joyce's writhing body. And then at Tara, and Rebecca, and Tara again.

Tara took a deep breath. "Don't mind us," she said. "We've—we've got this under control."

CHAPTER THIRTY-FIVE

Sam looked down at the body on the floor and tried to wrap his head around this entire mess.

This room was weird. It was like an old barn on the outside, but it'd been beautifully converted inside. To be honest, it made Sam a bit jealous. First thing that struck him was this sort of place would be absolutely ideal to hole up in. It had a functioning roof that hadn't fucking caved in, for one. It was warm. Warmer than *anywhere* Sam had felt since the blackout. It smelled nice, too. Which was irrelevant at this point; he was fully aware. But still, it got him thinking. They were on the road north—a journey that suddenly seemed completely irrelevant in the grand scheme of things considering everything that'd happened so recently. But he was definitely keeping his eye out for places that would be suitable.

He didn't like the idea of walking right into some sort of community or merging with some kind of group. That didn't suit him somehow.

He preferred the idea of being on his own.

As few people as possible.

Hell, this lot was enough as it was.

But as he stood in this room, he looked down at this woman. Lying on the floor. Old. Grey hair. Had this creepy smile on her face. Wide, piercing eyes.

She was quite clearly dead.

Blood trickled down from her mouth, right down her chin. A little bubble of snot clung to one of her nostrils. Her face was a weird shade of blue. He didn't know what'd happened to her; only she had a syringe sticking in her neck. Some weird fluid inside it that didn't look good at all. She smelled—Stunk of Dettol, or bleach, or something like that.

And at the other side of the room, sitting on a bed, he saw Rebecca, and he saw Tara.

They were sitting upright. They were both pale. They didn't look well. Didn't look well at all.

He could see the blood on Tara's chest. And he could get a sense of what had happened here.

She must've attacked this woman. For whatever reason, she must've attacked her.

But Sam couldn't stop wondering.

Was this the woman Tom told him to speak to about the drugs he so desperately seemed to want?

And if so... what the fuck were they going to do next?

Because this woman was supposedly the key to getting Marky back.

And now here she was.

Lying dead in front of him.

"So," Sam said. I've got to ask the question. "What the hell happened here?"

Tara and Rebecca told him. They told him about getting stuck in the mud. They told him about how they'd both woken up in separate beds and rooms, and both told the other was dead. Neither of them had any idea how long they'd been here. Only that at first they trusted this woman. They believed in her sincerity.

And then, when they questioned it... when they picked a little beneath the surface... they found something they didn't like at all.

"Any news on Marky?" Rebecca asked.

"Yeah. About that."

He told her about Lydia, Tom, and everything that happened at the house. The drugs.

"And he told me there was a batty old woman here who could help us find these drugs. Who'd tell us where they were. If we... asked nicely."

He looked down at the woman, Joyce.

Tara and Rebecca looked down at her, too.

"Well," Tara said. "Somehow, I don't think this bitch has anything else to say. So we're gonna have to figure out a plan B."

"I guess we've only got one choice," Sam said. "Find the drugs. Get them back to the house. And hope to fuck that cunt isn't bluffing."

They left the room. Searched the hallway. Tried every door. The place was weird. It was far vaster than it looked. He kept finding keys everywhere. It was like there was a weird trail.

But the more he looked, the more Sam realised he was struggling.

There was no sign of the medication.

And considering this woman seemed to have tons of syringes and medication, he couldn't wrap his head around it.

"Any luck?" he called.

Tara shook her head. Rebecca... Rebecca was struggling. Wasn't walking much at all. She didn't look in a good way. Looked pale and looked really sick.

"You okay?" Sam asked. Putting a hand on her arm, instinctively.

She nodded. "I will be."

And then it hit Sam suddenly. Fuck. He'd forgotten. He'd completely fucking forgotten. "Tristan," he said. "And... and Leonard. And Millie, too. Wayne's kid. They're outside. I'm sorry. I was... I was so caught up in all this, I should've mentioned."

Rebecca's eyes widened.

The love he saw in her eyes when he said Tristan and Leonard's names was both heartwarming and sad.

He saw himself in Tristan's place.

Saw himself as the man Rebecca loved.

And then... and then he let go, and he felt happy for her.

"Go on," he said. "We'll... we'll keep on looking here."

She took Sam's hand. Squeezed it. Tight. "Thank you, Sam. I'm... I'm glad you're okay."

"You too."

They held eye contact for just a few seconds longer than Sam knew was normal.

And then she walked away.

Down the corridor.

He watched her every step.

Watched her feet walking along those floorboards.

He watched as she walked out of this barn, and he took a deep breath.

He knew it was time to keep searching.

He knew he couldn't just give up.

He knew...

And then he saw something.

Up the corridor.

A piece of flooring Rebecca had just walked on.

It moved.

And not naturally, either.

He walked over to it.

Walked right over to it.

Slowly.

Crouched down.

Lifted it.

And he realised something.

It was a hatch.

A fucking hatch.

He pulled it further up.

Saw a padlock.

A padlock that... looked like the mystery key he'd found. The one he couldn't place. The one Joyce had in her pocket.

He put the key in the padlock.

Held his breath.

Turned it.

The padlock clicked open.

He pulled it away, and he lifted the hatch.

Pushed it open and looked down into the damp, dusty darkness below.

"Sam?" Tara said. "Is that... Are the drugs down there?"

A smile of relief stretched across Sam's face. "Something much better."

CHAPTER THIRTY-SIX

Tristan stood outside the farmhouse and wondered where the hell Sam was—and what the hell that scream was.

It was getting late. Today had absolutely flown by. It felt like so much had happened. Marky's disappearance. The incident in the house with that Tom bloke and the rest of his crazy friends. Coming out here with Sam in search of the drugs to give those junkies, and then hearing that scream. That was a little while ago now.

And here he was.

Still outside, with Millie and Leonard.

Still standing here and waiting to discover the source of that scream.

Still wondering whether his worst fears were going to be realised.

He looked down at Leonard and Millie. Saw them both looking up at him. Millie, in particular, looked especially curious.

"You okay?" Tristan asked. Trying to be calm. Trying to seem like he was in control. But all the while, he was scared. He was afraid.

He was trying his best to seem like a man who knew what he

was doing, a man who could look after his son and look after this girl, too, while deep down, he knew he was incapable.

Millie looked away.

"It'll be okay," Tristan said. Trying to reassure her. And trying to reassure his son in the process. "They... they'll be here soon. Sam'll be back here. And we—and we can think about getting back to normal then, right? On carrying on our journey."

"Where's Mummy?" Leonard asked.

Tristan didn't know what to say. Rebecca *had* been gone a while. And it was beginning to worry him.

But what was there to worry about?

Most people weren't psychos and nutters, right?

Sure. There were a few in that house. They'd bumped into a few more than was ordinary today.

But they were the exception to the rule.

Right?

He hoped so. He really did hope so.

He pictured them returning to the house and finding Tom and his band of freaks there, waiting for her.

And the thought of it made him nervous.

The thought of it made him wonder if he was making the right call here.

Or if he should be thinking about heading back immediately.

He looked around at the fields. At the dark grey skies. He looked at the crows and the seagulls swooping down, feeding on the worms. He saw the rain sprinkling down from above. And in the distance, far ahead, he could see the rough direction where the house was.

Just looking at it made his stomach turn.

He'd never been a particularly confident guy. He'd always had some sense of imposter syndrome in his life. A sense that he was just playing at being confident and playing at being in control.

But the truth was, he was afraid.

He was very afraid.

And it was a fear that had always followed him, right through his life, from childhood to adulthood.

He never pictured himself as a man with a kid. He always thought he was separate somehow. Like he was on the main stage and everyone else living their normal lives were just players.

And there were those turning points in his life, of course.

Meeting Rebecca and having Leonard being perhaps the most major.

But standing here right now, he got the sense he was on the cusp of another major turning point.

Because he needed to decide what he had to do.

Stay here and wait for Sam.

Go in there and search for him and the source of that scream.

Or go back to the house and face Tom and his people before his wife could get back there.

He stood there, heart racing, his mouth dry.

Held on to Leonard's hand and Millie's, too.

He didn't feel strong.

But he felt... stronger.

And that was something.

For now, it was enough.

It had to be enough.

He took a deep breath and turned around to face the farm when he suddenly saw them walking towards him.

There were a few of them. And Sam was there. Sam, and a dog he didn't recognise.

But there was only one person here his eyes focused on.

And that person was walking right towards him.

"Rebecca," he said.

"Tristan."

"Mummy!" Leonard shouted.

Tristan ran towards her, still holding the hands of the other kids. He held her tight. She looked weak. She looked like she was struggling. She looked completely exhausted.

"What happened to you?" Tristan asked.

"We don't have to talk about it now," she said.

"But—"

"It's okay. I'm here now. You did good. See? You did good."

And hearing her say those words... he knew it was pathetic, but it made him realise that he was stronger than he thought.

He was more capable than he thought.

He looked around at Sam, and that's when he noticed something else.

Millie.

She'd let go of his hand.

She'd...

He looked over to Sam and Tara's side and saw someone else.

A little boy.

He looked pale, and he looked dazed.

But he was smiling.

Smiling as his sister held her arms around him.

"Marky," Tristan said.

He looked up at Sam, and he smiled at him. Tears stung his eyes. The ex-husband of Rebecca had gone in there, and he'd brought his wife back for him.

And now here was Marky, too. Wayne's kid. The one they'd been looking for.

"I don't know what her game was," Sam said. "But she was sick. Very fucking sick. But we've got Marky now. And you know what that means?"

"What?" Tristan asked. Holding Rebecca and Leonard's hands tight.

A flicker of anger flashed across Sam's face.

"It's time to go back to the house and have a word with our squatting friends."

CHAPTER THIRTY-SEVEN

Tom stood in the doorway of *his* house and was starting to get nervous about this whole thing.

It was getting dark. The day had disappeared with the click of a finger. It was chilly out. Felt like winter was on its way. Or maybe he was just cold 'cause he was nervous. He always got cold when he was nervous—used to get nervous whenever he went to the theme park with his dad as a kid. Didn't want to go on the rides, so always ended up in this shaking fit. Realised in years later that it wasn't just the cold—it was nerves. But that's how it manifested itself in him. That's how it surfaced.

He stared over towards the farm. Saw its dark silhouette right there in the distance. Maybe something had happened there. Maybe something had gone wrong.

He was getting twitchy. A knot in his stomach tightening. A sense of nausea building right in the middle of his chest.

And he knew why.

He knew exactly why.

He'd been a heroin addict for as long as he could remember. And by that, he didn't mean he was shooting up as a kid. Just his memories from when he was younger were... blurry, somehow.

They weren't as vivid. He could *remember* things from his child-hood. But he couldn't *feel* them.

He'd only started feeling when he'd started heroin.

He knew it probably wasn't a great idea for his life prospects. No Class A drug was, was it?

But he got to a point in his life where he didn't really give a shit about his life prospects.

He gave a shit about *living* life. Not living for someone else. Not slaving away in some corporate hell to earn himself a measly pension which he might not even be healthy enough to enjoy anyway.

So he'd chosen another path.

He stood at the door and clenched his teeth, which were already ground down to stumps. If this Sam bloke got him the methadone, he'd be eternally grateful.

But there was a problem.

And that problem was this Marky kid.

Tom didn't know where the fuck he was. He didn't have a fucking clue where he was. But Sam and Tristan had gone out there on the premise that they would be reunited with him and get him back.

What the fuck was Tom going to do about that?

About the fact he didn't have anything to give him?

Anything at all?

"I hope you've got a plan."

It was Gilly. She was right by his side. She was tough. Real hard. The hardest person here.

She stood by his side and looked outside, arms folded. She was shaking a little, too, picking at a scab on her arm, which looked like it was bleeding heavily and weeping.

She didn't look well. But none of them were well, really, were they?

They were all addicted.

They were all sick.

They were all desperate, and they were all weak.

"He'll... he'll understand," Tom said.

"He will?" Gilly said.

"It's—it's desperate fucking times. He's got to understand."

"Oh, yeah. Sure. You've sent him right into the fire. You've got him doing a job for you. You've promised payment. The ultimate payment. And you're just gonna turn round and say, "sorry, chump, but thanks for the shit," and expect them both to just walk away? Nah. Nah, that ain't gonna work. Not at all."

Fuck. As much as Tom didn't want to admit it or accept it... she was right.

She was right, and he knew she was right.

They were gonna have to think differently.

They were gonna have to think bigger, somehow.

Outside the box somehow.

"Have you got any ideas?"

Gilly shrugged. Puffed out her lips. "Well we know one thing for sure."

"What's that?"

"We don't have his payment. And either he's gonna come back here with our payment, or he's gonna come back with nothing at all."

"So?"

Gilly shrugged again. "I just... I mean... there's no police about anymore. We're in the middle of nowhere."

"What're you suggesting?"

Gilly sighed. "I just... If something were to happen to them. It's not like it'd... like it'd come back to bite us. Is it?"

Tom couldn't believe what he was hearing. What Gilly was suggesting.

She was suggesting kidnap.

She was suggesting... even worse.

Murder?

"They're—they're just people looking for a place to stay."

Gilly rolled her eyes. "They're establishment pricks. You said it yourself last night. The kind of people who've been trampling us down their whole lives."

"We—we don't know that."

"Look. All I know is that I want to survive. And if we don't think proactively here... we aren't going to survive. We've got nothing to offer them. Nothing. So we've got to face it. Unless we make the first move, if you think they're just gonna play by the old rules, then you're wrong. You're very wrong."

Tom hated that she was right. 'Cause, she was. Sam and Tristan weren't going to just come back here and play nicely.

They were going to be fuming when they found out about Marky.

Which meant they had to try something else.

Whether he liked it or not... they had to try something else.

And it wasn't something Tom really wanted to think about.

"What do—what do you suggest?"

Gilly stepped towards Tom.

She put a cold hand on his shoulder.

Leaned into his ear.

And the she told him.

She told him exactly what they were going to do.

CHAPTER THIRTY-EIGHT

Sam saw the house up ahead, and he felt completely and utterly torn about what he would do next.

It was night. Darkness had set in. And it felt particularly dark, too. A thick cover of cloud overhead making it even worse.

And just seeing that house right there in the distance.

Seeing it and wondering whether going back there was the right thing.

Because they had Marky.

They'd found Marky, they'd freed Tara and Rebecca, and they were all here together.

Only... they weren't all here.

There was him. Tara. Rebecca. Tristan. Leonard. Millie and Marky. And this weird dog called Murph, which had latched onto them.

But there was no Wayne.

And there was no Harvey.

He knew they could just bypass the house. Go around the back. That was probably the most sensible move right now. After all, Tom and his bunch of pricks didn't have a clue about Marky after all. They'd used him. Sent him to that farm on a journey that could've been dangerous, and they had nothing to give back in return.

He wanted to make them pay for that. Wanted to make them suffer for that. Wanted to *punish* them for that.

But at the same time... would it not be best to just leave them alone?

"What're you thinking?" Tara asked.

Sam sighed. "I'm thinking I'm torn. Between what's right and what's... well. What's *really* right."

"I get you," Tara said.

"How about you?"

"Huh?"

"It's not like I'm the leader or anything. Everyone's got a right to an opinion here. What're you thinking?"

Tara scratched her head. "I mean... I understand. Harvey and Wayne. We need to find them. And Tom and his people... they've done a really fucking shitty thing to us."

"I'm sensing a 'but'."

"But..." Tara said. Filling in that silence between them. "I mean... we don't need to shake the wasp's nest any more, you know? They wanted the drugs. They're right there, sitting in that farm. They've got exactly what they want right there."

"It just feels—"

"Wrong. I know. But it is what it is. So they've got what they wanted. We've got Marky back. We're all here. We're all alive. We're just missing... Harvey and Wayne. We go to the house, play nicely, and tell them we've found Marky and let bygones be bygones instead of letting things get violent... then maybe we'll have a chance at finding them. Maybe they'll communicate."

Sam wasn't sure. He was kind of all for making these fuckers pay for fucking with them.

But at the same time, he fully saw the logic in what Tara was saying.

He knew she was right.

"What about their perspective, though?" Sam said.

"What?"

"Think about it. They're expecting us to get back here with their shit. Only they don't have their part of the bargain. They're going to be thinking about that. And they're going to be planning for their own eventualities, too."

"Then what do you suggest?"

Sam looked around. Saw Tristan and Rebecca. Marky, Millie, and Leonard there in front of them. Marky was stroking the dog, Murph. They were here. They were together. And considering all they'd just been through... they looked happy.

"We need to make them know somehow," Sam said.

"What?"

"If we're really going down this route... they need to know we're waving the white flag. They need to know we've found Marky."

"And how are we going to do that?"

"I can only think of one way," Sam said. Looking right at Marky.

"Are you sure that's... are you sure that's safe?"

Sam looked at her. "What else do we have?"

Tara shook her head. "Unless..."

She glanced up at Sam, then. Looked right into his eyes.

"Oh," he said. "I see where this is going."

"It doesn't have to be you."

"Of course it has to be me."

"And why's that? Because you're the big, strong leader?"

"No. Because of how you look at me like it has to be me."

Tara shook her head. Puffed out her lips. "I just... I wish there were another way. And it doesn't have to be you. Really."

"No," Sam said. "It... it does."

He looked around at the house, and he saw the only road opening up right before him.

He was going to go to the house.

He was going to go there alone.

He was going to tell them how shit was going to progress from here.

And hopefully—hopefully—it was going to be enough to keep him alive.

To keep *everyone* alive.

"I still can't believe I'm thinking in terms of life and death," Sam said.

"Huh?"

He shook his head. "I just... It's weird. How quickly things change, isn't it? You see a little death... and suddenly, your life is turned upside-down. Completely upside-down. Everything changes. All so quickly."

She looked into Sam's eyes. Stared right into them. It looked like she had something to say. Like she had something on her chest.

"It wasn't... it wasn't my first time," Tara said.

Sam frowned. "What?"

Tara rubbed her arms. She looked nervous. Really edgy all of a sudden. Like she was going down a road she didn't want to go down. A road she was terrified about going down.

But a road she had no choice *but* to go down.

"I... When I was a kid. I... I was... I was at a park. With my sister and her—and her friends. Older kids. I wanted... I wanted to get home. I wanted to get back home ' Mum told me we had to be home for nine. But Emily, she—she didn't want to go because there was a boy there she fancied. And she wanted me to stay there. She didn't want me to leave.

"I remember... I remember going for a walk and—and seeing him in the bushes. Oliver, he was called. One of the older kids. I never liked him. He always... he always made me feel weird. Uncomfortable. He said things to me that made my skin crawl.

And then there he was. Right there, by the pond. And I was on my own.

"He smiled at me. He—he told me to come over and sit with him. But I just... I felt weird. So I—I started to walk away. And then I started to run. And... and he followed me, and I pushed him into the pond and..."

Her eyes were wide. She was somewhere else. Somewhere else entirely.

"He banged his head on a rock in the water. I could see all this blood taking over the murky water. The brown turning red. I tried... I tried to pull him out. I shouted—I shouted for help. I held... I held on to his hand. He held on to my arm. Only..."

She stopped.

Shook her head.

"I didn't help him. I was... I was holding him down. I wasn't letting him up out of the water. Because—because I wanted him gone. I wanted him... I wanted him to disappear."

"Shit," Sam said.

"When Emily and the others got there, his eyes were still open, but he'd stopped struggling. I thought... I thought he was going to just go to the hospital and that they'd bring him back and everything would be okay. That—that he wouldn't cross me again. Or... or that he'd wake up and he'd tell what happened. That I'd go to prison.

"So... so when I found out he'd died... at first, I didn't feel shocked. I didn't feel guilty. I felt... I felt relieved."

Sam listened carefully. She'd been carrying this with her for years. Her whole fucking life, as far as she could tell.

"Jonno was the only person I ever confided in about this. Emily... I think Emily knew. And it's part of why we were never close after that. Jonno held the knowledge over me like a prison. Like a trap. And now... and now he's gone... as much as I am sad about it. As much as I miss the early days... I feel like—I feel like he was my final thread to what happened."

"And now you've just gone and opened another one. I hope you don't kill me too."

Tara laughed. She actually laughed.

And Sam laughed with her.

"That's why I like you," she said.

Sam felt his cheeks heating up a little. "I like you too."

"That's why... that's why I liked that kiss."

He looked at her, into her eyes, and he felt all kinds of barriers rising.

He felt all kinds of walls propping up all around him.

He felt the tension building to a breaking point.

That moment, that kiss, and how they'd not spoken of it again since.

He felt himself holding back.

Felt himself resisting.

He didn't want to open up another door of pain.

He didn't want to...

And then he just said, "Fuck it," and he leaned in to kiss her.

But before he could reach her lips, that's when he heard it.

The footsteps.

He looked around.

Saw...

Shit.

Tom was standing there.

His four crooks were standing there.

And they weren't alone.

They had Wayne.

Beaten.

Bleeding.

And on his knees.

The woman beside Tom held a knife to Wayne's throat.

"So," Tom said. "Are you gonna tell us where our shit is? Or are we gonna have to... to escalate things?"

CHAPTER THIRTY-NINE

Sam saw Tom standing there in the middle of the road, and he really fucking hated that this bastard had the audacity to interrupt what was quite an important bloody moment.

It was dark. The air was cold. And Tom was standing here with his hands on his hips. He wasn't a big guy. To be honest, it was kind of comical seeing this little douchebag acting like the tough man.

And if it wasn't for the woman by his side having a knife to Wayne's neck, he wouldn't have hesitated about doing anything at all.

But unfortunately, the woman by his side *did* have a knife to Wayne's neck.

And that was problematic.

"Well, this is an interesting approach to take," Sam said. "Especially since you were lying about Marky."

Tom tutted. "We did what we had to do. How about your part of the bargain?"

"The shit you need is back at the farm."

"That wasn't the deal."

"Look," Sam said. "We did what you wanted us to do. And

considering you didn't even have any fucking thing for us in return, I'd say that's pretty fucking fair of us."

"The deal was you *brought* the drugs to us," Tom said.

Sam felt torn. Torn between honesty and vagueness. He could tell them that the drugs were destroyed. That there was nothing left of what they wanted.

Or he could keep on going down the road he was going down.

He wasn't sure which path was the most productive.

Or which was the most dangerous.

"Look," Sam said. "That old woman you told us about turned out to be far battier than you advertised. Our friends here... our friends here got into some kind of shit with her. She isn't here anymore. But we're... we're right back to square one. You have Wayne. And you have my dog. We can walk away right now, and it'll be over. Completely over."

"But you didn't bring what we asked you to bring."

"We would've done," Tara said. "If we could."

Tom narrowed his eyes. As too did the woman with the blade to Wayne's throat. "What's that supposed to mean?"

Sam opened his mouth, went to hold up the lie, and he sighed. "Look. We found... we found these drugs you sent us out there for."

"You did? Then where are they?"

He looked around at Tara. Then at the others.

A gamble, he knew.

But a gamble he had to take.

"They were already gone," Sam said.

Tom narrowed his eyes. "Gone?"

"Trashed. Destroyed. Nothing left. You can see what scraps you can get out of it if you want. But honestly. I wouldn't even bother. I don't think it's worth getting your boots dirty."

Tom looked stunned. The others looked stunned, too. And Sam knew this could really go either way. He would either be rewarded for his honesty or pay for it.

He looked over at Tom, and he knew he needed to be ready.

He needed to be prepared.

"He's speaking bollocks," the woman beside Tom said.

"Why would I be speaking bollocks?" Sam said. "I coulda told you they were all over there. That there were tons of them. All I want is you to hand Wayne and Harvey over and... and we're done here. We can move forward."

The woman beside Tom shook her head. Kept that knife to Wayne's neck. Wayne was gagged. Sam could see him moving his lips underneath that tape across his mouth, but obviously, he couldn't speak. He was trying to move, too, but the more he shifted, the more that woman pressed the knife down.

Pressed it down so hard that Sam could see blood trickling down his neck.

"Listen," Sam said. "I'm not saying we're ever gonna see eye to eye. We're different. I accept that. But we've got two paths we could go down right now. And there's nothing to be gained from taking the violent path here. Trust me."

Tom opened his mouth. Closed it again. Looked like he was trying to say something. Like he was torn.

"Put the knife down," Sam said, looking at this woman. "Let Wayne go. Let my dog go. We walk away. And you... Well. You do whatever the hell you want. Just treat Lydia with more respect than you have been. And if you don't... let her come with us."

He saw Tom's eyes widening a little.

He could see right away that he was softening.

That he was coming around to Sam's argument.

Because what was the point in any of this?

This was no way out.

Any escalation at this point... it was pointless.

Truly pointless.

And he could see that Tom was seeing that now, too.

He could see a path opening up, right in front of them, for the pair of them.

"Okay," Tom said.

"What?" the woman said.

"I said—I said okay. We... we hand them over. And this... this ends. This ends now."

Sam felt a wave of relief.

They were going to let Wayne go.

They were going to let Harvey go.

And they were going to be allowed to make the final stretch of their journey, at last.

"Let him go," Tom said. His voice shaky. Quivery.

The woman shook her head.

"Gilly," he said. "Let him go."

Gilly looked at Tom.

She looked at the other people.

And then she looked back.

Right at Sam.

She looked into Sam's eyes, and she smiled.

"We were promised a delivery," she said.

She pushed the knife harder against Wayne's neck.

"And they failed to deliver."

Wayne's eyes widened.

Tom's eyes widened.

And it all happened so fast.

Gilly buried the knife into Wayne's throat.

She sliced.

Sliced hard.

Blood spurted everywhere.

Splattered right down his chest.

"No!" a voice behind Sam shouted.

It might be Tara.

It might be Rebecca.

It might even be the kids...

But he couldn't think.

He couldn't take anything in other than the scene before him.

Wayne fell to the ground.

Tears rolling down his cheeks as blood spluttered out of the gaping wound in his neck.

Tom looked on in horror.

Everyone looked on in horror.

Everyone, except this Gilly.

"Now walk the fuck away," Gilly said. "Leave. Right this fucking second. Unless you want this dog here to be next."

But Sam didn't want to walk away.

He didn't want to leave.

He didn't want to—

"Go!" Gilly shouted.

Raising her knife.

Walking over towards Harvey, who sat there, wagging his tail.

And the worst thing?

The worst thing of all?

Sam was so worried about anything happening to Harvey that right now, in this horrifying moment—this moment where they had no weapons, nothing to fight with, nothing to defend themselves with, nothing to attack with—he nodded.

He nodded, and he started walking back.

Staring at Harvey all the time.

At him sitting there, wagging his little tail.

Ears back as he wondered what was going on.

"Go," Gilly said.

And he saw Wayne. He heard the crying of the children and the swearing and the shock of the people around him, and he saw Wayne.

His head was raised.

He was bleeding out of that wound in his neck.

Badly.

And he was stretching a white, shaking hand out.

Like he was reaching for someone.

Like he was reaching for the kids.

"Go," Gilly said.

Sam looked into Wayne's eyes.

Right into Wayne's eyes.

He wanted to tell them he'd protect them.

He wanted to tell him he'd avenge him.

But in the cold, horrifying terror of the moment, Sam could only do one thing.

He turned away with his people in tow, and he walked off into the night.

CHAPTER FORTY

Sam saw the signs for Lancaster, and he knew they were getting closer to the moment their paths diverged.

It was morning. They'd been walking all night. All night, through the darkness. All night, through the cold. All night, through the rain. He wanted to stop. Wanted to rest. But he knew the second he stopped and rested meant more time with his thoughts.

More time to think about what'd happened.

More time to feel the guilt and pain for what he'd witnessed.

He saw the buildings up ahead. The city of Lancaster was never the busiest in the country, but right now, it was silent. He could see the student accommodation buildings rising over the landscape. He could see the cars winding their way all the way up towards the city. He could even see Williamson Park standing tall in the distance. He used to go there as a kid with his grandparents. Get an ice cream. Ride along the path on his bike. They were good memories. Warm memories. Summery memories.

But he didn't feel anything good anymore.

He didn't feel any warmth anymore.

He only felt guilt and shame for what had happened.

He tasted bad breath and vomit. He'd been sick quite a bit. He constantly felt nauseous and weak. He felt like he was on the verge of collapsing at any given moment.

But just as long as he was here to see the people he was with got to some kind of safety... that was enough.

After that... after that, he didn't know where the road led for him.

Only that he couldn't be on it.

He looked around.

Saw Rebecca and Tristan walking just behind. Leonard on Tristan's shoulder, sleeping.

And he saw Tara.

She was holding both Millie's and Marky's hands. Both of them had their heads down. Lowered. Staring at the ground. That dog, Murph, right beside them.

They looked shattered.

Completely and utterly shattered.

He looked at those kids, and he kept on thinking about their stepdad.

About that awful, horrible moment.

That totally unnecessary moment, too.

Wayne, on his knees.

That woman, Gilly, slicing open his throat.

Making him bleed out all over the road.

Right in front of the kids Wayne had gone so far and fought so hard to care for.

It was brutal. It was ruthless. And it was so, so fucking wrong.

He thought about these poor kids. They'd lost their mum. And then they'd lost the man who was pretty much a dad to them. They were on their own. Truly on their own.

And Sam had stood there and made the wrong call.

If he'd been tougher... he could've taken on Tom and those junkies.

If he'd gone with his Plan A... this might not have happened.

He'd made the wrong call. And it had cost Wayne his life.

He looked at Murph, and he thought about Harvey, then, and it turned him cold right from the inside.

He'd walked away.

He'd walked away from his fucking dog.

His dog that he loved.

Loved more than... fuck, he loved Harvey more than anything.

But that woman. That Gilly.

She was threatening him.

She was threatening Harvey.

And Sam just couldn't have anything else happening to someone he loved.

He especially couldn't have anything happening to Harvey.

He just couldn't.

"Sam."

A voice. Tara.

He felt his jaw tensing. He didn't want to talk to her. Didn't want to talk to anybody. "We're almost at the Arnside turn. Not much further to go."

"I don't—I don't want to talk about Arnsi—"

"And I don't want to talk about anything," Sam snapped. "I... I want to get you lot somewhere... somewhere safe. And then..."

"And then what?"

"I don't want to talk about it."

Tara was quiet, then. And for a moment, as he kept his head down and waded along the waterlogged road, he thought she might've actually got the message. He needed his alone time. He needed his space. He needed—

"Sam, I—"

"I don't want to talk about it," Sam said. Turning around. Snapping.

He saw the look on the kids' faces.

He saw the way they looked up at him.

Like they were scared.

Like they were afraid.

All of them looking at him like they'd seen his true colours.

Like they were seeing the real *him*.

He stood there in the middle of the road.

Saw Tara.

Saw Rebecca.

He saw the kids, and he saw Tristan, and he saw this dog, Murph.

And as he stood there...

As he stood there, he didn't see a way forward for him from here.

He didn't see a way forward at all.

He just wanted Harvey back.

He just wanted his dog back.

He just wanted... the guilt to go away.

He looked away.

"I'm sorry," he said. "But I can't... I can't do this anymore."

And then he turned, and he walked.

"Sam?"

But Sam didn't stop walking.

He didn't stop walking towards those woods alongside him.

He didn't stop for any of their shouts or any of their calls.

He just kept on going.

Kept on going.

Kept on going and going until he was so far away that he couldn't hear their shouts anymore.

Kept on going until he was alone.

CHAPTER FORTY-ONE

Sam wasn't sure how long he'd been walking through the woods, into the darkness, when he heard the footsteps right behind him.

He sighed. He had no idea if it was one of his people or not, but let's face it, it probably was. He was in the middle of nowhere. He'd just stormed away from his people. And as much as he knew it was probably a bit melodramatic and probably wasn't the most helpful move to make, he didn't see himself belonging with those people anymore.

He'd let them down.

He'd let those kids down.

They were better off without him.

As for Harvey...

Those junkies would falter eventually. But until then, the thought of them with their junkie hands all over him... no. It didn't sit right. It didn't fucking sit right one bit.

He didn't know what his fucking plan was.

But he needed to get his dog out of there.

He wasn't going to let him fall.

He was going back alone, and he was—

"Sam."

A voice.

A voice right behind him.

Not Tara's voice.

Not even Rebecca's voice.

Not the voice he expected at all.

He turned around, and he saw Tristan standing there in the darkness.

He walked over to him. He didn't have any look of judgement on his face or anything like that. He just half-smiled at Sam. "Weird place and weird time for a walk."

Sam sighed. "Just... just leave me alone."

"So you can go wandering into killing yourself? No thanks. Nobody wants that."

"What the hell do you care anyway?"

"What the hell do I care? Hmm. Strange question. Maybe I actually think you're a decent bloke. Maybe I don't want to see you destroying yourself. Maybe I think our group is better when you're around. Stronger when you're around. And... and maybe I look at you and I think Jesus, you're everything I should be in a man, and even though that should fucking *terrify* me because you used to be married to the love of my life... I don't want to see Rebecca unhappy. And I know she will be unhappy if you walk away. If you destroy yourself. So too, will Tara. So too, will the kids. And... and so too will I."

It was a strange speech. One that Sam didn't expect from Tristan. And by the look on Tristan's face, it wasn't something he'd planned or anything either. It was kind of free-form—kind of stream of consciousness.

But there was something sincere about it.

There was something earnest about it.

And there was something in what he said that struck a chord.

"I don't know where we go from here, quite frankly," Tristan said. "I know... I know the *logical* solution is to keep heading north. To keep on seeking shelter and safety. But... but at the same time... at the same time, I don't think it's right."

"What's not right?"

"Letting those bastards get away with what they did. And leaving Harvey there in their hands."

Sam nodded. "I appreciate that. And that's exactly why I have to go back."

"Not alone," Tristan said.

"What?"

"I said... I said you aren't going back there alone."

"So, what? You're walking away from your wife and your kid so you can help her ex-husband on his little revenge missing to get his dog?"

"Not just him."

Another voice.

From the trees.

Rebecca.

He saw Rebecca.

And then he saw Tara.

And then he saw the kids, and this dog, Murph.

And before he knew it, he realised he wasn't alone at all.

The pair of them weren't alone at all.

"Wow," Sam said. "How long have you lot been here watching and listening?"

"It doesn't matter," Tara said. "What matters is that you know we're with you."

Sam shook his head. "I'm touched. Really, I am. But there's absolutely no way you're coming with me. Not after we... Not after what happened to... to Wayne. I can't... I can't do that. Not again."

"Well unlucky for you, sugar-tits," Rebecca said. "Because it isn't your choice."

She stepped forward.

And Tara stepped forward with her.

The kids and Murph walked up, too.

"You're one of the strongest people I've ever known. If not *the* strongest," Rebecca said. "Sorry, Tristan. But even you'll admit you're a damp squib compared to him."

Tristan raised his hands. "Guilty as charged."

"The Sam I know wasn't a quitter. He wasn't someone who gave up. And he definitely wasn't reckless, either. Going back alone is reckless. It's careless. And you know damn well you can't do this alone. Smart, you might be, but we're going to need all the brainpower we have if we're going to get Harvey back. And screw the people who killed Wayne over. Royally."

Sam looked into her eyes. Shook his head. He didn't know what to say. Only that he was actually... quite touched.

"I don't want anything to happen to you. To any of you."

"Well, unlucky," Tara interrupted. "Because whether you like it or not, we're with you."

She smiled at him.

And for a second, for just a second, he smiled back.

Rebecca again. "So are we going to go back? Or are we going to stand here in the dark woods and mope for the rest of the night?"

Sam looked at these people.

Then he looked around in the direction they'd come from.

In the direction of the house and Tom and his junkie friends.

He felt his fists tighten.

He knew what he had to do.

He knew *exactly* what he had to do.

CHAPTER FORTY-TWO

Sam stood on the hill and looked down at the house, and he knew what he had to do.

Exactly what he had to do.

He could see the sun rising in the distance. It was nice—nice orange glow about the place. And something was calming about it. Something reassuring about it, considering all he'd been through. All his people had been through.

And considering the fact he was looking down towards the bastards who had stolen his dog, who had murdered Wayne in cold blood... and for what?

For their junkie fix.

Yeah. He felt pretty fucking angry; that much was clear.

But at the same time... at the same time, he looked around, and he saw the people standing beside him.

He saw Tara.

He saw Rebecca.

He saw Tristan.

Leonard.

Millie.

Marky.

And Murph, the dog.

He saw all these people standing here with him, and he knew he wasn't alone.

He'd given up not long ago. Accepted he was on his own. That he was going to have to go on a suicide mission to get Harvey back.

But it didn't have to be that way.

Even if he knew he still had to be careful, even though he knew the fewer people sneaked in, the better... he was going to be more careful.

He looked down at the house. It was quiet. No movement at all. Those junkies would probably be off their faces on whatever shite they'd got their hands on.

And Sam knew what he had to do.

He knew he had to play it cool.

He knew he couldn't go charging in as he'd originally planned.

He knew he had to be more careful.

And that meant waiting.

That meant being patient.

Even though every iota of his being wanted to go storming in there, get Harvey out, and destroy this lot... he knew they would be on edge right now.

Waiting.

Which meant Sam had to be patient, too.

He had to bide his time.

He had to wait for the perfect moment to strike.

And then when he did... these fuckers weren't going to know what hit them.

"What are you thinking?"

It was Tara. She was here, right by Sam's side. Standing there alongside him, looking down at the house.

Sam felt his fists tighten.

He took a deep breath of the cool air.

"We wait," he said. "And then when the moment's right... we step up. We get Harvey back. We fight."

He looked into Tara's eyes, and for the first time in what felt like a long time, he smiled.

"We avenge Wayne. And we crush these fuckers. Once and for all."

CHAPTER FORTY-THREE

Tom sat in the house, and he was starting to feel really fucking hungry.

It was late. He had no idea how long had passed since all that shit with that Sam prick and the others. No idea how long had passed since Gilly cut that Wayne fella's throat and spilled blood all over the road. It could be days, or it could be weeks. He had no fucking idea anymore.

The only thing that really mattered was that he was still alive.

And that felt like it counted for quite a lot these days.

He was in the house. Sitting in the lounge. It reeked of sweat and piss, some of which was probably his own, he was well aware. He was freezing cold. His jeans were loose. Felt like he'd lost a bit of weight in the last few days, which was obvious, really. He wasn't eating as much—and he didn't use to eat a lot as it was. He felt dehydrated. He felt exhausted.

And he couldn't stop looking at the dog sitting there in the middle of the lounge and thinking about how shitty he felt about what happened with his owner's people.

"We can't go on like this." It was Gilly. She had a tendency to come out with bold, dramatic statements like that lately without going on to back them up with any kind of logical conclusion.

And usually, Tom just sat there and let her say shit like that. 'Cause, to be honest, as much as it pained him to admit it... he was beginning to fear Gilly a bit.

She was erratic. That much was clear.

And he was worried that it felt like the leadership in this group had shifted away from him and over to her.

He didn't like that. Not one fucking bit.

She sat there shaking her head. She looked so pale. So grimy. So rough. "We're fucking starving here. And what're we actually doing about it?"

"You could suggest something, you know," Tom said.

He saw how she glared over at him, and he kind of regretted speaking up right away. "What was that?'

He wanted to back down. But fuck. He wasn't going to be afraid of her.

He was going to stand up to her.

He cleared his throat. Took a deep breath. "You're always complaining about how shit things are. But I never hear you coming up with any viable solutions."

She puffed out her lips. Smiled a little. "Think you'll find I'm the only one who had the balls to stand up to those people."

"And for what?"

"What was that?"

Tom knew he should stop. But he was on a roll now. He was on a roll, and he couldn't stop himself. "You go on about how you were the only one to stand up to them. What was it for? Where has it got us? *What* has it got us?"

Gilly licked her lips with that long, serpent-like tongue covered in angry little spots. "It's got us respect."

"Respect?" Tom said. "You killed a man. And you stole a dog. What sort of respect has that got you? Really?"

"Do you have a problem with my methods?"

"You know what? Maybe I do."

He stood up. Went to walk out of the room.

And right on cue, Gilly stood up too.

She stood there, right in his way.

Staring at him with quivering, twitching eyelids.

She had a knife in hand.

A knife still covered in the blood of that man she'd killed.

"Because if you have an issue with my way of doing things," she said. "I'm sure we could all have a very serious discussion about your role in this group."

Tom shook his head. "You fucking *live* here because of me."

"I live here because of Lydia. This house isn't yours. It's mine as much as it is yours."

"You fucking bitch."

Gilly lifted the blade.

Pressed it to Tom's neck.

"Careful," she said. Her eyes lighting up. "You wouldn't want me to slip, would you?"

Tom looked around at the others.

The other three people.

Three people he'd let live here.

Three people he considered his *friends*.

He looked at them all with their heads down.

Not looking.

Choosing not to pay attention.

And he saw it clearly now.

The hierarchy had shifted.

Things had changed.

And he wasn't as powerful as he used to be.

He wasn't as powerful as he thought he was.

He wasn't powerful at all.

Gilly moved the knife across his neck. So close to cutting through his skin.

"But we don't want any trouble," she said. "Do we?"

He shook his head. "No."

"What was that?"

"I said... I said no."

She smiled, her eyes lighting up a bit. Psycho bitch. "Good," she said.

She walked over to Harvey, then.

Stroked him.

He lowered his head, and he growled.

Clearly didn't like her.

The hackles on his back rising right on end.

"Don't you worry, Harvey," she said. "If we don't find a good lot of food soon... you'll provide for us. You'll make the ultimate sacrifice. Won't you?"

Tom felt sick.

He knew what Gilly was getting at as she crouched there, stroking Harvey with the blade.

"Good boy," she said. "Good little boy."

She looked up at Tom, and she smiled.

He forced himself to half-smile back.

Because what could he do?

He was a prisoner in a home that wasn't even his own.

There had been a silent coup.

And he had no power here.

No power anymore.

He stood there in the darkness of the lounge, and he stared down at Gilly and Harvey as the smell of weed filled the air, and he had no idea where things were going to go from here.

He didn't see the figure standing outside the window.

Standing there in the darkness.

Staring in.

Watching.

CHAPTER FORTY-FOUR

Sam waited until all had turned quiet in the house before opening the back door and stepping inside.

It was unlocked. Of course it was fucking unlocked. These people were idiots. Dangerous idiots, maybe, but idiots all the same.

And as much as he wanted to go in all guns blazing, so to speak, he knew that he couldn't do that right now.

He knew he needed to be more careful than that.

He needed to go inside, and he needed to find Harvey.

And then he needed to get Harvey out of here and leave.

The time for revenge would come.

But they were going to have to be patient before they got there.

This was just phase one.

And he had to bear that in mind.

He stepped into the dark kitchen. It stunk in here. Reeked of weed, sweat, and vomit. He could hear something coming from the living room. Sounded like talking at first, which made him a little nervous.

And then he realised it was snoring.

He clutched onto the knife he was carrying just in case he ran into trouble, and he stepped into the kitchen.

He had to find Harvey. He was hoping he'd just be right here downstairs waiting for him. But truth be told, he didn't expect that. He'd been watching this group for four days now. Staking them out. And they always kept Harvey with them. Always.

Which... wasn't going to make getting him back as easy as he would like it to be.

He walked through the kitchen anyway, being careful to be extra quiet. He didn't want to make any noise. Didn't want to draw any attention to himself. Even though, based on the luck he'd had since the power went out so far, he was fully expecting to draw attention to himself. Fully prepared for that god-damned eventuality.

He looked around the kitchen. No sign of Harvey.

Which meant he was going to have to check the lounge.

The lounge, then...

Upstairs.

He felt nervous about the prospect of heading upstairs. It wouldn't be as easy to escape if he got caught up there.

But the time for nerves getting away was over.

He walked further down the hallway towards the lounge door. Knife in hand. He knew what the plan was.

Get Harvey.

And get out.

Deal with revenge at another time, if convenient.

But there was also something else here, too.

He'd agreed with the others—who were waiting outside on watch—that if taking out these people made for a cleaner run at Harvey, then he shouldn't hesitate.

As for why he'd come in here alone after that grand talk about unity four days ago, well. That was a part of unity, too.

He didn't want to risk the safety of anyone in his group. Going this alone was a wiser idea. They all agreed to it, reluctantly.

There was no use more than one of them coming in here.

It was better if it was just him.

Better if they were outside, on watch.

He walked over to the lounge, and he stopped outside the door.

His heart pounded.

He held his breath.

He didn't expect to find Harvey in here. Because it was never going to be that easy, was it?

But maybe, just maybe, he'd find some luck today.

He pushed the door open and saw two of them in there.

The two he hadn't really had any dealing with. Not the woman who'd killed Wayne. And not the bloke with the face he'd bashed. The other two.

Lying on the sofas.

Snoring.

He saw them lying there, and he heard a creak upstairs. It could be a footstep. Or it could be the wind.

And as he looked at them, seeing no Harvey in tow... he felt torn.

On the one hand, he wanted to go over to them.

Cover their mouths.

Slit their throats.

But on the other...

He turned around, and he walked out of the lounge, clicking the door shut as quietly as he could.

And then he grabbed a sweeping brush that was on the floor. Looked like it'd swept up a bunch of vomit and smelled like it, too.

He stuffed it behind the door to wedge these bastards in.

And then he stepped back.

Turned around and looked at the stairs.

He hadn't seen Harvey downstairs anywhere.

So there was only one place he could be.

"Come on, Harv," Sam whispered. "Aren't you dogs supposed to have a good sense of smell or something?"

He walked over to the foot of the stairs. Looked up into the darkness.

His heart raced.

His chest was tight.

His mouth was dry.

But he knew he had to go up there.

He knew he had no choice.

"Well," he said. "Here goes nothing."

He walked up the stairs being careful to be as quiet as he possibly could. It was windy outside. And every few steps, the stairs creaked, making him wince.

But he could hear snoring upstairs, too.

He could hear then, and he felt right in the belly of the beast now.

He gripped that knife.

He had to be ready.

He climbed to the top of the stairs. Looked around at the three doors facing him.

All of them closed.

Fuck. If Harvey started barking now...

"That'd be a bloody typical time to decide you're a guard dog, wouldn't it?"

He walked over to the first of the doors on the left. Saw the bathroom. Empty. A real shithole. Shit all over the sides of the toilet, which reeked. The bath was all stained, too, with a combination of shit and piss and God knows what else.

And syringes, too.

Syringes everywhere.

He turned around, and he walked up to the next door.

Pushed it open ever so slightly.

Still holding his breath.

Still bracing himself for whoever and whatever he might find.

In this room, he saw the man with the fucked up face.

He saw the man who was supposedly the leader, Tom.

And he saw the woman.

The creepy psycho woman who'd slit Wayne's throat right in front of his children.

He wanted to go in there right now and bury his blade into her body again and again.

But he remembered the task at hand.

He had to remember the task at hand.

He stepped out of the room and heard a floorboard creak underfoot.

He froze.

Froze solid.

That floorboard was loud.

The snoring stopped.

For a second, for just a second, time stood still.

They'd heard him.

They'd heard him, and they were going to come out here and...

And then he heard the snoring starting again, and he knew he was safe.

For now.

He walked away from the room, and he looked at that final door.

There was only one place Harvey could possibly be, and it had to be in there.

There or up in the attic.

He walked over to this final door.

Pushed it open.

Slowly.

He could hear something in here, too.

Mumbling.

Someone mumbling something.

And it made the hairs on the back of his neck stand right on end.

Until he realised who it was.

In this room, sitting cross-legged and upright on the bed, Sam saw Lydia.

She was staring into the darkness.

Mumbling all sorts of things.

And she was stroking something in front of her.

"Harvey," Sam said.

Harvey lifted his head.

He wagged his tail.

And as much as Sam didn't want him to make a noise... he immediately leaped off the bed and came bounding across the room towards him.

"Hey," Sam said, hugging him as he wagged that tail and licked his face. "Good lad," he said. "Good—good lad. You be quiet now. You settle now, okay? You can have all the fuss you like when we get out of here, huh? How's that sound? That sound good?"

He ruffled Harvey's fur and tried to get him to calm down when he saw Lydia sitting there on the bed.

Looking over at him.

Smiling at him.

"You made it," she said. With a whisper. Which was a relief. 'Cause Sam had braced himself for her to let out a scream or something—something to alert the rest of the dickheads here to his presence.

He could see a tear rolling down Lydia's cheek in the light of the moonlight. "I'm glad... I'm glad you made it. And now—and now you've got to go."

Sam stood up. Harvey by his side. "I'm not leaving you behind."

He walked over to Lydia when he saw something else.

She wasn't smiling at him anymore.

Her eyes were wide.

She looked... afraid.

"You don't have to worry, Lydia," Sam said, placing a hand on her bony shoulder. "It's going to be okay now. Everything's going to be okay. I promise. I..."

And then he realised something.

Harvey growling.

Lydia's staring.

And the faint sound of footsteps right behind him.

He went to turn around when suddenly he felt something against the back of his head.

Hitting him.

Hard.

And knocking him to the floor.

His ears rang as his face collided with the floor.

He tasted blood.

He turned around as he tried to grip onto consciousness, as Harvey started growling when he saw him standing over him.

Hammer in one hand.

Lantern in the other.

It was one of Tom's people.

The one he'd punched in the garden a few days ago.

Smiling.

"Hello, you," he said.

Lifting his hammer.

"I wondered when we were gonna get to finish what we started..."

CHAPTER FORTY-FIVE

Sam lay there on the floor and looked up at the fuckwit staring down at him holding that hammer, and he knew he was in deep shit.

The bedroom was dark. He could hear ringing in his ears. He could hear Harvey growling. He could hear Lydia through the ringing, just about, muttering under her breath.

He could taste blood, strong on his lips. He felt like his head was all fuzzy like his attention was drifting. Like he was slipping away but desperately trying to cling on...

He couldn't let himself slip away.

He needed to stay alert.

Needed to stay ready.

As he clutched onto the...

The knife.

Fuck.

He'd been holding the knife. Gripping it tight.

But he couldn't feel it in his hand anymore.

It was gone.

Fuck.

He must've dropped it when he got cracked over the head.

He looked around the room for it, around the darkness, barely lit by the old-fashioned lantern this prick was carrying.

The lantern illuminating the smirk on his face.

"You thought you could just come back here, did you?" the man said.

He pulled back his foot and buried it deep in Sam's stomach, making him wince.

And then, before Sam could catch his breath, the man reached down.

Dragged him up and onto the bed.

Pinned him right down.

All the while, Lydia just whimpered and muttered things.

And all the while, Harvey just growled.

Whined and growled.

He wanted him to help him.

Needed him to help him.

But at the same time... he didn't want Harvey to put himself in danger right now.

He knew pricks like this wouldn't hesitate about hurting a dog.

The man pinned him down on the bed. Squeezing his throat. Sam gasped for air, tried to get a grip on the bloke's neck in turn, but it was no use.

He was pinned down.

He was trapped.

He was in deep fucking shit.

And the way he saw it right now, there wasn't a thing he could do about it.

The man looked down at him. Smirk widening across his face.

"I wanted to finish you off in that kitchen so fucking bad," he said. "And I shoulda done. I can see it now. Tom... Tom was weak. Gilly ain't weak. She's strong. And we listen to her now. We listen to her. Not to him."

He tightened his grip even more.

So tight that Sam could see colours pulsating in his vision.

So tight that he could feel himself drifting… drifting… drift…

No!

He felt his eyes widen.

Felt a burst of energy and a burst of strength fill his body.

He wasn't lying here and being screwed over by this bunch of weak cunts.

He was going to get out of here.

And he was going to take Harvey and Lydia with him.

He grabbed the man's hands.

Grabbed the back of those hands as hard as he could.

Dug his fingers into them and pulled him away.

He felt himself holding those hands there.

Those shaking hands hovering in the air.

He saw the man smiling as he crouched over him.

Laughing.

And he knew why it was.

It was because it was only a matter of time before Sam's resistance faltered again.

And he knew it.

They both knew it.

"It's admirable, really," the bloke said, possessing a more ambitious word than Sam thought he'd even have in his lexicon. "When people are pinned down, when they know damn well they are defeated… still they keep on fighting. Still they keep on resisting. When really they're just prolonging the pain for themselves."

Fuck. Had this cunt swallowed a thesaurus?

Either way, Sam held on.

Felt his muscles weakening.

Felt time running out.

He looked over at the lantern on the bedside table.

The hammer beside it.

Too far too reach.

Too far to…

And then he got it.

An idea.

An idea flashing in his mind.

An idea that he knew was dangerous.

An idea that he knew was an almighty risk.

But the only idea he had left.

He looked at that lantern. Then back up at the man. Right into his smirking face and at his eyes.

"Any last words?" the man said. "Cause I ain't waiting around for Tom. And I ain't waiting around for Gilly. You're mine, mate. You're mine. And you're finished."

Sam stretched out for that lantern with his foot.

Stretched his toes as far as he could until he felt the hot side of the lantern holder against his toes.

And then he looked right up into the man's eyes again.

"Watch where you leave your weapons," Sam said.

The man's eyes widened. "What..."

And Sam kicked the lantern off the side of the bedside table.

It all happened so fast.

The flames.

The heat of the flames as the lantern burst across the floor.

The yelp of this guy as the flames seared his leg.

The loosening of his hands.

And the chance Sam knew he had.

He leaped up onto the bed.

Grabbed the hammer.

Grabbed the man by the scruff of his neck.

"I wanted to show you mercy," Sam said.

He pulled back the hammer.

"But you don't deserve it."

The man's eyes widened. "Please—"

Sam cracked the hammer against the man's head.

Hard.

So hard the man's eyes rolled into the back of his skull right away.

So hard he fell onto the flames covering below.

He let out a little scream as he lay there on that bed of flames.

As he twitched, blood spluttering out of his mouth, out of his head.

As the fire quickly began to spread around him.

Far, far quicker than even Sam intended—because it was only supposed to be a momentary distraction, not a full-blown blaze.

But Sam stood there on the bed.

He stood there with Lydia by his side. Hands over her eyes.

He stood there as Harvey nudged his head against Sam's leg.

He stood there, and he looked down at the twitching body beneath him as the flames began to fill the room and as the smell of smoke began to clog up the air.

And as he stood there, watching as the flames stretched over towards the door in front of him... he realised something.

Something very stark.

He was trapped.

And he was fucked.

All of them were fucked.

CHAPTER FORTY-SIX

When Tristan saw the amber glow upstairs, he knew Sam was in deep, deep trouble.

It lit up out of nowhere. First, there was total darkness. Then, a slight glow of a torch. And then, the sound of commotion, the sound of fighting, the sound of scrapping, the sound of conflict.

And Tristan knew that wasn't good news. Sam was in there, on his own, and any sounds of fighting and confrontation could only mean one thing: trouble. The junkies had woken up. They'd spotted him. They were onto him, and he was in danger. Big, big danger.

He stood there outside the house in the darkness of night. A little sprinkling of rain showered down on him, nowhere near as bad as the torrential storms they'd faced over the last few weeks. The air was cold, and he was shaky. Shivery. Part of it was adrenaline, he was sure. Part of it was nerves.

The biggest part of it was fear.

And urgency.

Because as he stared up there, through those dirty old

windows of this decrepit old house, he got the feeling that he would have to do something.

He couldn't explain the way he felt. But he could only describe it as a sort of... inevitability.

A sense that everything had been building towards this moment.

A sense that right now, his life only had one purpose, and that purpose was somewhere right here in front of him.

He just didn't know what it was *exactly* yet.

"Do you—do you think we should do something?" Tara asked. "We can't... we can't just stand here. While... while he might be in trouble."

Rebecca lowered her head. She squeezed Tristan's hand. "We —we stick to the plan."

"We can't just leave him—"

"Sam's strong," Rebecca said. "Stronger... stronger than even I gave him credit for. And I knew he was strong. He'll... he'll make it out of this. He has to make it out of this."

"And if he doesn't?" Tara asked.

Rebecca looked at her. Right into her eyes with that wide gaze.

She took a deep breath.

"He'll make it out."

Tristan looked at Rebecca.

He looked at Tara.

And he looked at the kids, too.

The kids, and this dog, Murph.

Millie.

Marky.

And his Leonard.

He saw them, and he knew he needed to survive for their sakes, if for nothing else.

He knew he needed to be strong for them.

He knew he had to be there for them. Millie and Marky as

much as Leonard, his own son, at least for the time being, until they found somewhere to resettle.

And... if there was one thing Tristan prided himself on, it was that he was a good dad. He was caring. And he didn't say that in an arrogant or over-confident way. He just *was*.

He'd cared for his younger brother when they were kids, and he was sick with cancer.

He'd cared for Dad when he lost a leg and couldn't walk anymore.

He'd cared for himself all the while, feeling grateful even to be alive at all, healthy and well.

Tristan was good at caring for people.

He might not be the conventionally strong man... but he *was* strong in a way that many men weren't strong.

He was emotionally strong.

And right now... right now, Tristan could feel that emotional strength calling on him to do something different.

Something he didn't want to do.

But something he *had* to do.

That's when Sam appeared at the window.

He was holding something. He looked like he was covered in blood and sweat. The amber glow behind him was bigger than ever. It was quite clear that there was some sort of fire in there.

"You need—you need to take him," Sam shouted.

"Sam?" Tara said. "What—what's—"

"The place. It's... it's on fire."

"Sam—"

"You need to take him. Okay? Harvey... Harvey'll fit out this window. He'll make the drop if one of you catches him right now."

"What about you?" Tara shouted. "What about... what about you?"

Sam didn't answer.

He didn't have to answer.

He just stared out of the window at Tara and then at Rebecca with Harvey in his arms.

"I'll... I'll be okay," he said. His voice cracking just a little. Just enough to reveal his vulnerability. "Just... just catch him. Catch him, and I'll be okay."

Tristan stood there, not quite believing this was happening.

He stood there, and he watched as Tara shook her head.

As Rebecca... as Rebecca cried.

He tightened his grip around her hand.

Felt the coldness of her fingers squeeze back.

Because whether he liked it or not... Sam was the man she'd loved once.

And when it was your first real love... you never quite fully moved on from them.

You always held something for them.

And this must be painful for her.

So, so painful for her.

He watched as Tara ran over towards Sam.

As she stood there, waiting for Sam to drop a rather reluctant-looking Harvey out of the window.

He watched as he lowered Harvey down.

As he said something to Tara, as she stared back up at him, crying.

And he watched as Sam dropped his "good boy" out of the window, down towards Tara below.

Tara caught Harvey. Tumbled to the ground in the process.

But she had him.

She had him in her arms.

Harvey jumped out of her arms right away.

He backed up, looked up at Sam. Started barking.

Barking right up at him in that window.

And Sam stood there.

Sam stood there as the orange glow engulfed the room behind him.

Sam stood there as the flames filled that room.

Sam stood there as the inevitable started to play out right before everyone's eyes.

The horrible inevitability.

He looked at Tara again. Said something to her.

Then he looked at Rebecca, who was crying quite heavily now.

"You're... you're a good woman," he said to Rebecca. "I'm sorry for the hurt I caused you. But I'm glad you've found Tristan. I'm glad you've found him. Because—because he's a good man." And then he looked right at Tristan. "You're a good man."

Tristan stood there. Looking right up at Sam.

He stood there as that amber glow turned to a white-hot brightness.

He stood there, and he waited for those flames to fill the room as Harvey looked up there, barking at the top of his lungs, and...

"No," Tristan said.

He tightened his grip around Rebecca's hand.

Turned around.

Looked right at her.

Saw her frowning at him through her tears. "Tr—Tristan?"

He looked at her, and he felt his eyes stinging. He felt a lump swelling in his throat.

He felt that sense of inevitability growing and growing to bursting point.

And he knew what he had to do now.

Exactly what he had to do.

As painful as it was... for Rebecca especially... he knew it was the right thing.

"I have to," Tristan said.

Rebecca's tearful frown grew. "What?

"I just... I love you so much. And I'll make this work. I promise I'll make this work."

He leaned over.

Kissed her right on her lips.

And then he turned around, and he hugged Leonard so tight.

"Daddy'll be back in no time. There's something... something he needs to do."

And then he stood up.

He looked at Rebecca, who stood there, shaking her head. Like she was clearly in disbelief about all this. "Tristan? What—what are you..."

"I'm doing what I have to do," he said.

And then he took a deep breath.

Tightened his fists.

"I love you."

And then he turned around towards the house, and he ran.

"Tristan!" Rebecca shouted. "Tristan, no!"

But as Tristan ran, tears in his eyes, as much as he wanted to turn round, as much as he wanted to go back... he knew he couldn't.

He knew he was on a path he couldn't change now.

He ran towards the house.

He ran towards Sam.

Because he wasn't giving up on Sam.

He was going into that burning house, and he was going to get him out of there.

Or he was going to die trying.

CHAPTER FORTY-SEVEN

Sam stood on the bed and stared out of the window as the flames engulfed the room, and even amid all these flames, he felt relieved.

He felt happy.

Because Harvey was okay.

Harvey was safe.

As were the rest of his people.

He looked around the room. Saw the flames all over the carpet. The smell of smoke was strong in the air, making him dizzy. You think you can imagine what it's like to be caught in a cloud of smoke. You always dismiss it, don't you? Assume you can just cover your mouth, and everything will be okay.

But it wasn't like that at all.

The smoke was sharp, like knives digging into his throat, scratching their way down into his lungs, slicing slowly.

And the worst thing was the cough.

When you coughed, it made the pain even worse.

It made those knives dig in even more.

Tearing away.

Slicing away.

He heard shouting from another room. He couldn't tell what they were saying. And he couldn't tell who it was.

All he knew was that he felt strangely... calm.

Strangely at peace.

He felt his head spinning. Tasted vomit in his mouth. He felt sick. So, so sick.

And yet... it was a calming kind of sick.

It was like falling under the spell of anaesthetic.

Slipping into sleep.

Harvey was okay, and his people were okay.

That was the main thing.

They were going to be okay now.

They were going to be...

And then he saw Lydia.

Saw her lying there on the bed.

Sitting upright and staring into space.

She looked like she wasn't suffering anymore.

Like she wasn't struggling anymore.

She looked... at peace.

Sam staggered over to her side.

He put a shaking hand to her neck as he coughed and spluttered in the smoke.

Felt for a pulse.

But he didn't feel anything.

His stomach sank.

It was too late.

Poor Lydia was gone.

He tumbled forward, then. Coughed up his guts. On the discoloured white bedding, he saw blood.

Specks of blood.

His head spun. He could see colours in his vision. He was so warm, and those flames were growing higher. He looked over at the door. At the flames crawling up it. He could get over there. He could climb over the burning carpet, and he could get through the door and...

He felt himself drifting.

And then he felt another sharp stab of pain right in the middle of his chest.

Another bout of coughing kicked in.

He spluttered up his guts all over the bed.

More bile.

More vomit.

More blood.

And as much as he tried to kid himself about how he could make it to that door, make it downstairs... he knew he was living in a fantasy world.

He heard shouting outside. Someone calling Tristan's name.

And as he lay there on this warm, comfy bed, he smiled.

That would be something, wouldn't it?

Tristan coming in here.

Saving him.

It was a funny thought. But it was a nice thought.

It was a thought he felt himself sinking further and further into...

Getting out of here...

And holding Tara's hand and...

It struck him, then.

Tara.

It was Tara who came to mind.

Tara who entered his thoughts.

For the first time, he could remember, his thoughts hadn't defaulted to Rebecca.

They'd defaulted to Tara.

He opened his burning eyes. Saw the bright flames. Saw the door.

And he wondered as he lay there next to Lydia's dead body if maybe he could make it after all.

If maybe he still had the strength in him to get out of here.

Because he had so much to fight for.

He had so much to *live* for.

He stretched out towards that door with what little strength he had in his body when he realised it was futile.

And it was ironic, wasn't it?

He wanted to live.

He finally, finally wanted to live.

And now he wanted to live—now he'd found someone to live for—he wasn't going to be so fortunate.

He wasn't going to be so lucky at all.

He lay there, a tear rolling down his face when he saw something.

The door.

That burning door.

Opening.

He stared at that door with his wide eyes.

Watched and waited for someone to step inside.

Tristan?

Could—could he have made it in here after all?

He watched and waited as his eyelids grew droopy, his chest started failing him, as he struggled for breath in a room that was rapidly running out of oxygen.

And then he saw him.

Walking through the door.

For a second, his hopes rose.

And then he realised who it was.

It wasn't Tristan.

But it was someone else he recognised.

It was... Tom.

Lydia's stepson.

Sam looked up at Tom standing there in the flames with his wide eyes.

He looked at him, and he knew this was typical. It was just fucking typical, wasn't it?

"Come on," Sam said. "Do—do whatever you... whatever you have to do." His voice failing by the second, growing more and more hoarse. "Finish—finish the job."

Tom stood there in the middle of the flames.

He looked at Sam, then at Lydia, then back at Sam again.

And then he shook his head.

He rushed over to Lydia.

Checked her pulse.

"Shit," he said.

"Now... now's not the time to start... to start caring."

He looked down at Sam, then. And Sam knew what was coming. This prick was going to piss on his grave, essentially. Anything to make him feel a bit stronger.

"Come on," Sam said. "Just—just get on with it. Just do it. If it's what... if it's what makes you feel stronger."

Tom looked down at him.

He took a deep breath.

And then he held out a hand.

Sam frowned. "What... What are you..."

"My people made your people suffer for far too long, pal. And I'm—I'm sorry. I'm so sorry for all the shit that's gone down here. I've made—I've made some bad choices. But I just... I just want to get this one right. So come on. Let's—let's get out of here. Let's get out of here now."

Sam looked up at Tom's hand. Still not quite believing anything that was happening.

But knowing full well, time was running out.

"Come on," Tom said. "Hurry. Before we run out of time."

Sam didn't want to trust him.

He didn't want to take his hand.

But he knew he didn't have a better choice right now.

He reached up and grabbed Tom's hand.

"Got to admit," he said. Rapidly losing his voice entirely. "This wasn't... this wasn't how I saw this going."

Tom pulled him to his feet. "Me neither. Now come on. Before..."

He stopped speaking.

And Sam didn't know what it was.

Not for a moment.

His eyes widened.

He opened and closed his mouth. Like he was trying to find the words for something he'd seen but just couldn't.

His hand tightened around Sam's.

Like a vice grip.

"Tom?" Sam said. "What..."

And then he saw blood trickling down his chin.

He felt the weight of his body tumbling forward onto him.

"No," Tom said. "N—I don't want... I don't want to die. I don't... Please."

And as Sam stood there, his head spinning, his body weak, he realised what had happened, and his stomach sank.

There was a knife in Tom's back.

And someone was standing behind him.

The woman.

The psycho who'd killed Wayne.

Gilly.

She looked at Sam with those piercing eyes, blood splattered all over her face, and she smiled.

"Hello, Sam," she said. "It's just you and me now."

CHAPTER FORTY-EIGHT

"Hello, Sam," Gilly said. Smile across her face, glowing in the flames. "It's just you and me now."

Sam lay there on the bed. It was dark and cold outside, but it was the total opposite in here. Bright. Suffocatingly hot.

Only... that brightness was growing weaker because of the smoke.

The thick smoke rising up all around him.

Gilly stood there. Smirking. Flames all around her. She had a knife in hand. A bloody knife, which she'd just yanked out of Tom's back. Tom lay twitching on the burning floor, right by the other bloke's side. Sam felt sorry for him. He'd been a prick. He'd caused some real shit here.

But at the same time... at the same time, he'd tried to make amends.

He'd tried to change.

And he couldn't hold that against him.

He could hear the floors creaking and crumbling all around him. Further away, he could hear shouting. He didn't know if it was his people outside or Gilly's people in here. In a way, it didn't matter.

Just as long as his people were okay.

Just as long as they were safe.

Just as long as they were far, far away from here.

The air reeked of smoke. He tried to hold his breath, but there was only so much he could hold it. He needed to breathe. But at the same time, he knew breathing too much would kill him.

The smoke would knock him out.

And then the flames would swallow him up.

If the smoke poisoning didn't kill him first.

Probably the more preferable option.

Gilly didn't seem affected. She didn't seem fazed at all.

She just stood there, sweat trickling down her pale face. Bloody knife in hand.

Looking right at Sam like she was enjoying this.

A psycho, that was for sure.

A real psycho.

"So this is what it comes to," Gilly said. "You could've just stayed away like I told you to. But you couldn't help yourself. And now look at the mess you've made."

She walked towards him. Over those flames, which were surely burning her.

Knife in hand.

Dripping blood.

"You don't deserve to walk away," Gilly said. "You made your choice. You're here. This is your bed. And you are going to lie in it. You deserve no better."

"You killed them for—for no reason," Sam said. Struggling to speak now.

"I killed them with very good reason," Gilly said. "I killed them because they threatened my home. They threatened *my* life."

"And how—and how has that worked out for you?" Sam asked.

Gilly smiled. Like she enjoyed this near-death sparring.

"The fact is... we're trapped here. We're both trapped here. And if I'm going down... then I'm taking you with me. You came in here. And—and you'll pay the price for coming back here. That's just... that's just how it is. That's just..."

She started coughing, then. Hands on her knees, shaking, coughing everywhere.

Saw her spit onto the floor.

And... and he saw something else, too.

Her hair.

It shifted a little.

Loosened.

Like... like she was wearing a wig.

She saw Sam was looking at her, and she rolled her eyes. "No point hiding it anymore, right?"

She pulled her wig away, revealing a bald head.

"Terminal cancer of the lungs," Gilly said. "So I'm not sure a smoke-filled room is great for me right now."

She coughed some more—Spat blood out onto the floor.

"To be honest, I don't know how long I had to live anyway. I could—I could go out in a miserable, agonising, depressing way. Or... or I could go out strong. I could go out fighting. I could go out... with drama. That's more *me*. And that's how it's going to be. So I thank you for that. Really."

Sam shook his head. "I wish I could say I'm sorry. But you've... you've hardly made the most endearing first impression."

Gilly actually laughed at that. "But I made an impression. Didn't I? People... people have a funny way of acting when they know it's all about to end."

"And how—and how has it made you feel?"

She looked up like she was thinking.

And then she looked back down at Sam.

"Free."

She lifted her knife.

Pressed it to his chest.

Right to his heart.

"I'm sorry it has to end this way for you," she said. "In another life, I have a feeling we might've got along."

She pushed against his chest, right between his ribcage.

"But you know how this world works. I can see it in your eyes. It's rough. It's harsh. It's unfair. It's... Well. That's life."

She pushed harder.

So hard against his chest muscles, he could feel the sharp end of that knife piercing through.

He thought of Tara.

He thought of Rebecca.

He thought of them both, and then he...

He saw movement.

A shadow.

Right by the door.

The door swinging open.

Tristan running in, over the flames.

Coughing.

Spluttering.

Hurtling towards Gilly.

It all happened in slow motion.

Gilly turning around, distracted by the sudden entry.

Sam reaching up and snatching that knife away from her.

Slashing her throat.

Seeing that look of shock in her eyes as she clutched her neck and she bled out all over him.

Seeing that... almost that look of *admiration* as she tumbled to the bed, covering the sheets in red.

He held her hand as she fell.

Held her tight hand as she choked on blood.

As she gargled.

As bubbles of blood burst from her lips.

He held her there as she looked up at him.

As she looked up at him with that smile.

Holding on to his hand.

"I'm sorry you lost your humanity at the end. But no matter... no matter what happens to me right now, I won't lose mine."

He held onto her hand as she twitched.

Held onto her hand as she struggled.

And he kept on holding onto her hand as she finally stopped struggling.

As she went still.

He looked up at Tristan.

Coughing.

Surrounded by flames.

And then he looked out, over at the window.

The window outside, where Rebecca, Tara, the kids, Harvey, and that dog Murph all waited.

He looked back at Tristan, who lay there on the floor, surrounded by flames.

And he nodded.

"Thank—thank you," Sam said.

Tristan opened his mouth, struggling to get the words out between the coughs. He was clearly struggling. Clearly in a bad way.

"Reb... Rebecca," Tristan said. "Leonard. Get... Get out. For... for them. For them."

Sam stood there in this burning house as it collapsed all around him, and he held on to Tristan.

And in this burning house... he looked at the door and knew what would happen here.

He knew no matter how hard he tried exactly what was going to happen here.

He held on to Tristan.

Tristan held on to him.

And as the flames surrounded... he closed his eyes, and he felt the smoke fill his lungs, and the heat cover his body, and he knew what happened next.

Exactly what happened next.

He thought of Rebecca.

He thought of Harvey.

And more than anything, he thought of Tara.

He kept his burning eyes closed as he crouched there next to Tristan, and he held on to him tight.

"Thank you," Sam said. Knowing they were both screwed. And wishing Tristan hadn't come in here and condemned himself, too.

But at the same time, being so overwhelmed by emotion.

"Thank you for... for being a good husband to her," Sam said. "Thank you for..."

And then his voice failed, the smoke made him dizzy, the heat intensified, and he felt himself drifting and drifting and...

CHAPTER FORTY-NINE

Tara stood outside the burning house and watched as everything fell apart.

The glow of the flames contrasted with the jet black of night. The rain had stopped, but the air was cold and windy. She hadn't seen anyone come out of the house. And she thought about running through the door herself. Thought about running in there and trying to find Sam. Trying to find Tristan. Trying to get both of them out of there.

But then she saw the flames completely covering the door, and she knew it was no use.

She knew it was over.

She heard Rebecca crying beside her, trying to keep composed. She could see her holding Leonard, hugging him, telling him everything was going to be okay. And she could see Millie and Marky there with Harvey and Murph. Both staring at this burning house and looking at the horror before them.

And she felt so bad for them. So bad for all of them.

All of this loss.

All of this pain.

And here she was, amidst all the panic and all the chaos, all she could think about was Sam.

That she'd seen him.

She'd seen him for the last time.

And now he was gone.

She stood there, and she shook her head. They should've done something. They shouldn't have let him go in alone. They should've tried to help him.

She went through all of these cascades of emotions and thoughts and feelings, but in the end, the only thing she could truly feel was despair.

Total despair.

Total loss.

She was going to miss him so much.

She looked at Rebecca. At Leonard. And she thought about the horror of what she'd just had to witness. Of what she was going through right now. Her husband was gone. The father of her kid was gone. And her ex-husband was gone, too.

Her life up in flames right before her eyes.

And the kids...

Millie and Marky.

They had nobody left. They already had nobody left.

But now, yet another part of their lives had fallen right before them.

The strong foundations they needed in their lives now more than ever were collapsing right before their very eyes.

And it was so, so fucking sad.

She looked over at the kids, standing there together.

And as much as Tara wanted to go in that house, as much as she wanted to go searching those flames for Sam... she knew those kids needed someone so dearly right now.

She walked over to them. Putting a hand on Rebecca's shoulder as she passed, so she knew she was there for her.

And then she walked over to the kids.

She looked down at them. And it wasn't just those two staring at the house with sad eyes. It was Harvey, too. He was sitting there so patiently, like a good boy. Panting. Whining. Occasionally even howling.

Like he knew Sam was in there.

And like he was just waiting for him to come out.

Tara crouched down. Swallowing a lump in her throat and taking a deep breath of the smoky air.

"It's okay," she said. "I... I promise this is going to be okay."

She was here for these kids. She had to look out for them. Had to look *after* them.

And then the most remarkable thing happened.

Millie stepped forward.

She hugged Tara.

And it was the words she said that touched her more than anything.

"It's okay," she said. Stroking Tara's back. "We—we're here for you."

Jesus fucking Christ, this kid. She was sweet, and she was brave, and she was so, so mature.

Tara tightened her grip around Millie. "And I'm here for you too. For both of you."

"Promise?" Millie said.

"Always"

She held her tight, and she felt her warmth against her body when suddenly she heard something behind her.

A voice.

"S—Sam? Tristan?"

Rebecca.

It was Rebecca.

Tara heard Harvey barking then.

Saw Murph barking too.

Something had got their attention.

Something had caught their eye.

She turned around and saw something right there in the doorway of the house.

A dark silhouette. Impossible to see his face with the flames behind him.

But there was no doubting who it was.

There was no doubting it whatsoever.

And when Tara saw who it was... she felt her body filling with relief and hope and joy, all in an instant.

"Sam," she said.

She saw him standing there. Then staggering out of the flames. A few of those flames burning his jacket.

He was carrying something.

Carrying something as he walked away from that building.

Carrying...

"Daddy," Leonard said.

He went running up after his mum, along with the dogs.

And as Tara watched Sam walk out of this house, she realised the kids were right.

Sam was holding Tristan.

For a second, for just a second, she felt panic.

Total panic.

Tristan's eyes were closed.

He looked...

Well.

He looked *dead*.

She saw Rebecca run over to him.

Saw her walk right up to his side.

Saw her speaking to Sam as he lay Tristan down on the grass.

"Tristan," Rebecca said. "Come on, love. Come on. Wake up. You're going to be okay. Wake up."

Tara saw him lying there.

Lying motionless on the ground.

She saw him lying there, and she saw her fate right there, in front of her.

"Come on, you silly bugger," Rebecca said, tears streaming down her cheeks. "It's—it's going to be okay. I promise it's—I promise it's going to be okay."

Tara stood there, and she felt that fear.

That fear of not being able to save someone once again.

That fear of losing someone she was trying to save once again.

But this time, she took a deep breath, and she pushed that fear aside.

"Wait there, kids," she said.

She ran over to Tristan.

Ran over to Tristan and looked down at him.

Lying there.

Burns on his skin.

Eyes closed.

"He..." Sam gasped. His voice sounded raw and raspy. "The—the smoke. It..."

She looked down at Tristan.

She saw him lying there, and she saw herself failing someone.

Failing someone all over again.

"Please," Rebecca begged. "Please, Tristan. Don't—don't you go on me. Don't you die on me."

Tara took another deep breath.

She felt her nerves dissipate right in that moment.

She felt herself focus right into this instant.

And then she crouched down, and she put her mouth over his.

She puffed into his lungs hard. She could taste the smoke on his lips and his breath. So much of it that it backfired into her mouth.

And then she backed away.

Did CPR.

One, two, three...

One, two, three...

And then breathed into his lungs again.

She kept on going. Kept on repeating the routine. Kept on

focusing right here in the moment as the house burned right beside her. As Sam watched on. As Rebecca watched on. As the kids watched on, and the dogs watched on.

"Please," Rebecca said. "Please…"

Tara reached down again.

She did compressions again.

She puffed into his mouth again.

And then she repeated the trick all over again.

She did another cycle when she looked over at Sam and saw that look in his eyes.

He saw the way he looked at her.

Saw the way he shook his head.

And as much as she hated it, as much as she didn't want to admit it… she could see that look in his eyes, and she knew what it meant.

It was over.

Tristan was gone.

She shook her head. She felt that sense of defeat surrounding her once again. She felt that sense of loss and failure swallowing her up all over again.

She looked down at Tristan, and she saw a man who didn't have anything left.

She saw a man who was gone already.

She felt herself preparing to accept defeat when suddenly, a wave of strength crashed through her body.

"I'm not giving up on you," she said.

She went in.

Went in for another round of compressions.

And then she went in for another inhalation of breath into his mouth.

"I'm not giving up."

She went in for another round of compressions.

One.

Two.

Three.

And then another breath into his mouth.

Still nothing.

She went in for that next round of compressions. A round she knew realistically was her last.

One.

Two.

Three.

Still nothing.

She looked down at Tristan's vacant expression, and she knew it was now or never.

She closed her eyes.

Went to inhale into his mouth.

And then, suddenly, out of nowhere, she heard something that changed everything.

Right there on the grass in front of her... Tristan coughed.

She opened her eyes.

Tristan was alive.

He was coughing, spluttering everywhere, but he was alive.

"Tristan!" Rebecca shouted.

She collapsed to the ground. Helped him sit upright. Patted his back as he coughed and rubbed his arms and shoulders as tears spilled down her cheeks. "You silly bastard," she said. "I thought —I thought I'd lost you, you silly, silly bastard."

Tara watched them both, and she felt her chest filling up with relief.

She felt her chest filling up with pride.

She felt tears rolling down her own face.

Tears of relief.

She'd done it.

She'd saved him.

She hadn't let him down.

She turned around, and she saw Sam standing there.

Looking right at her.

Smiling.

She looked back at him. Right into his eyes.

Smiled back at him.

Walked over to him and held out a hand to help him to his feet.

He took her hand.

And then he stood up, and he hugged her.

Tight.

She felt his warmth against her body, and she stood there in the heat of the burning house as it collapsed behind them.

She felt his warmth as Rebecca and Tristan reunited, as the kids clapped and the dogs barked, and she felt herself crying.

But not with sadness.

She cried with relief.

And she cried with joy.

She held on to Sam, and as the house crumbled and fell to pieces behind them, Tara felt safe.

She felt warmth.

She felt... loved.

She didn't know what the future held.

But right now, amidst this chaos, Tara had everything she needed right here.

CHAPTER FIFTY

One week later...

* * *

Sam saw the motorway stretching off into the distance, and he took a deep breath.

Because finally, he was beginning to feel like their journey was ending.

It was the middle of the day. A really sunny day at that. It was autumn, but there was a bit of warmth in the air. A bit of heat. He could hear birds singing, which was really bloody cliche on a nice day. But everything felt peaceful. Everything felt hopeful. Everything felt... optimistic.

Which was a weird thing to think when it'd been three weeks and the power still wasn't back on.

He looked at the road. The water had drained away from the floods at last. And that felt like a milestone in itself. The first days of the blackout had been marked by the floods, in a way. And seeing that water gone now... there was a strangeness to it. He wasn't sure what it was, but maybe a deep part of himself had been thinking that the power would be back online by the time the water vanished. An absurd thought, he knew. 'Cause he knew better than most that the power wasn't just coming back online any time soon.

But even so. You live in hope, right?

You live in hope that maybe, just maybe, your cynicism was wrong; that it was ill-placed. That the nation and the world are far more prepared for disaster than you think.

Turns out the exact opposite was true.

But you know what?

Standing here right now, Sam didn't care.

He looked around. Saw Millie and Marky walking along with Leonard and that dog, Murph. They were smiling. And it was nice to see. Especially after the horrors they'd been through the last couple of weeks. Losing their mum. Then losing their stepdad—or rather, the man who was pretty much qualified to call himself their dad.

And it wasn't going to be easy for them. The trauma was going to haunt them. The darkness would return, and when it did, they weren't going to always be able to snap out of it so easily. Especially not when they got a little older.

In a way, it was harder for Millie. She was older. She understood the way life worked a little more than her little brother. Or rather, the way *death* worked.

Marky... he was young. He was more resilient. And while it would be troublesome to get used to when he got older... for now, as much as he missed his mum and Wayne, they were doing their best job of rallying around him and looking after him.

As for Millie, Sam was so grateful she was just such a measured kid with her head screwed on. She was mature beyond her years. And thank God. He dreaded to think how difficult this would be for her right now if she weren't. She was going through loss and going through pain, and she was still right there, a rock by her little brother's side.

He looked around at Rebecca, Tristan, and Leonard then, and he smiled.

Tristan had some nasty burns from the fire back at the house. Clearly had some damage from the smoke, too. His voice wasn't quite there yet, and he found it difficult keeping up.

But he was alive.

That was the main thing.

He was here, and he was alive.

Sam thought back to the moment Tristan came running in after him while he was trapped in that burning house. He thought back to it a lot. He wondered if he would've done the same were the roles reversed. He liked to think he would. But *would* he, really? He wasn't sure.

Either way, one thing was for certain.

Tristan had nothing to prove to anyone about his strength.

But it seemed like he'd needed to prove it to himself.

He'd saved Sam's life.

He'd left that burning house with his own life intact.

And thank God.

Rebecca looked over at Sam. Smiled.

And Sam smiled back.

He always thought it would be weird reuniting with his ex-wife. He always thought it'd be a right shitter seeing her living her new life, moved on.

But seeing her with Tristan by her side and seeing that little boy between them... honestly, he felt happy for her.

Because she was happy.

And Tristan was a good man.

That's all he could possibly want for her.

And then he looked to his side, and he saw Tara standing there.

She looked gorgeous. Tired and greasy-haired, but gorgeous. Didn't they all look tired and greasy-haired? That was just the way people looked now. Better get used to it.

She looked into his eyes, and she smiled at him.

"You sure you're ready for this?" she asked.

He looked around at the road ahead.

And he saw it.

That community.

The little town they'd been following signs to for the bulk of the week now.

And he had to admit he felt nervous.

He had to admit he felt trepidation.

He had to admit it kind of went contrary to every logical and rational desire in his body right now.

But at the same time... it felt right.

A community.

For as long as it lasted... that was what he needed.

"You know what?" Sam said.

"Go on," Tara said.

"Ask me that question a few weeks ago—even just a week ago —and there's no way I would've said yes. But I've... I've realised maybe... maybe people aren't so bad after all. Not all of 'em, anyway."

He looked at her when he said those words.

Saw that smile on her face.

And he wanted to kiss her.

He wanted to kiss her so badly.

But that wall...

That wall in front of him.

Right between them.

He turned away before he could seize the moment as the fear took hold, and he looked over at that town again.

He'd conquer all his demons in time.

But for now... for now, this was a major one being conquered.

Standing by Tara's side.

His people behind him.

His new *family* behind him.

Facing a new start amongst new people.

New friends.

New enemies.

"Are you ready?" Tara asked.

Sam took a deep breath.

Nodded.

"I'm ready," he said. "How about you?"

"What's that supposed to mean?"

Sam paused. "Your parents. Arnside. Your family. What about them?"

Tara looked off into the distance. "You know... Maybe I'll see them again someday. I'm sure I will. I... I love them for who they are. But I..."

She looked back at Sam. Smiled again.

"Cheesy as it sounds... I think I have a new family now."

Sam felt a warmth in his chest. "Yeah. That does sound really fucking cheesy."

"Well, here's to real fucking cheese."

"Did somebody say cheese?" Tristan said.

Sam laughed. Tara laughed. All of them laughed.

He looked at Tara again.

Took a deep breath.

And then he walked by Tara's side, fingers brushing against hers, with Rebecca, Tristan, Leonard, Millie, Marky, and the dogs following behind.

It was time for a new beginning.

It was time for a new dawn.

END OF BOOK 3

Dawn of Survival, the fourth book in the World Without Power series, is now available on Amazon.

If you want to be notified when Ryan Casey's next novel is released—and receive an exclusive post apocalyptic novel totally free—sign up for the author newsletter: ryancaseybooks.com/fanclub